The Day the Playground Became Everyone's Place

Diversity and Inclusion

Willow Stone

Published by The Good Child Bookstore, 2024.

While every precaution has been taken in the preparation of this book, the publisher assumes no responsibility for errors or omissions, or for damages resulting from the use of the information contained herein.

THE DAY THE PLAYGROUND BECAME EVERYONE'S PLACE

First edition. October 7, 2024.

Written by Willow Stone.

Also by Willow Stone

Community and Society
Working Together to Build a Stronger Community
Small Acts of Kindness Make Big Differences
Overcoming Fear and Building Self-Confidence
The Bridge That Connected Different Worlds
The Lantern That Glowed with Honesty

Diversity and Inclusion
The Day the Playground Became Everyone's Place

Emotions and Feelings
Creating Safe Spaces for Everyone to Thrive

Table of Contents

Dedication

To all the children who have ever felt like they didn't belong—you are seen, you are valued, and you are important. This book is dedicated to those who create spaces of kindness and inclusivity, ensuring that everyone has a place to play, dream, and be themselves. To the friends who lift each other up and the communities that embrace every individual, may we continue building a world where everyone belongs. And to all the young readers, may you always believe in the power of inclusion and the difference you can make, no matter how small the idea.

Preface

When I began writing *The Day the Playground Became Everyone's Place,* I wanted to capture the importance of inclusivity and the power of community. Playgrounds are more than just spaces for fun—they are microcosms of society where children learn about friendship, fairness, and working together. Too often, though, some children feel left out, whether due to physical abilities, different interests, or simply because they don't fit into a specific group.

This story is about the journey of a group of friends who recognize that everyone deserves to feel included. By working together, they create a space where every child—no matter their background, abilities, or personality—can find joy in play. My hope is that readers will be inspired by Ora and her friends' efforts, and will be encouraged to create inclusive environments in their own schools, neighborhoods, and beyond.

Chapter 1: The Divided Playground

Sunnyhill Elementary's playground was a lively place, but not everyone felt welcome. There were different zones, and each one seemed to have its own set of rules, invisible to adults but clear to the children. The "Big Slide" was where the fastest and boldest kids played, and only the bravest dared to join. The "Soccer Field" was dominated by children who played every day, their skills so sharp that any newcomer felt out of place. In the "Quiet Corner," a small patch of grass under a shady tree, the quieter kids sat, watching but never participating in the games. Then there was the "Swing Set," where kids took turns—well, some did, but others hogged the swings, leaving others behind.

Ora stood in the middle of the playground, watching. She had always been a curious and kind-hearted girl. Her brown eyes sparkled as she observed her classmates. She loved playing on the swings and chasing her friends on the soccer field, but lately, she had started to notice something: not everyone was having fun.

In the far corner of the playground, she saw Althea, a girl in a wheelchair, sitting by herself. No one invited her to join the games, and she couldn't easily reach the areas where everyone else played. Ora also noticed Sami, a boy who seemed shy and always stood on the sidelines. He looked like he wanted to join the soccer game but never did.

"Why is it like this?" Ora wondered. "Why can't everyone play together?"

The thought stuck with her. After school, she brought it up with her best friends: Remi, Kiva, and Dano. The four of them always played together and had fun, but Ora felt something tugging at her heart.

"Have you noticed that some kids never play with us?" Ora asked.

Kiva tilted her head, her braids bouncing. "Yeah, but maybe they don't want to."

"I don't think that's true," Remi chimed in. "I saw Sami watching us play soccer today. He looked like he wanted to join."

Dano nodded. "And what about Althea? I've never seen her playing. It's like she's always left out."

Ora's heart ached. "I think we should do something about it. It's not fair that only some kids get to have fun."

"But what can we do?" Kiva asked.

Ora thought for a moment, then her face lit up with an idea. "What if we made the playground a place where everyone could play? We could create new games that everyone can join, no matter how fast they run or whether they can use the swings."

Ora's idea felt huge, like a towering oak tree that started from a tiny seed. But now that seed had been planted in her heart, and it was ready to grow. As she and her friends sat in a circle on the grassy field near the swings, they began to talk about how they could make the playground a place for everyone.

Remi was the first to suggest something. "We could start by creating games that don't need running, or at least games where speed isn't the most important thing. That way, kids like Sami won't feel left out."

Dano nodded. "Yeah, and maybe we can make use of the places nobody really plays in. Like the big tree at the edge of the playground. What if we made that into a special spot for a game that everyone could play together, even kids who don't like running around?"

Kiva leaned forward, her eyes brightening. "Or what if we invent a new game entirely? One that includes things like throwing, or maybe using teamwork so that everyone has a part to play, no matter what."

Ora smiled as she listened. Her friends were beginning to see what she saw, the potential for change. The playground didn't need to stay the way it was—segregated by unspoken rules and groups that only some children could join. It could be a place where everyone felt included, where no one was left out because of who they were or what they could or couldn't do.

"We can't do this all at once," Ora said thoughtfully. "But what if we start small? Maybe tomorrow we can try a new game and invite Sami and Althea to play with us."

"What game?" Dano asked. "We need something really fun to get everyone interested."

Ora thought for a moment and then clapped her hands. "How about 'Treasure Island'?"

"Treasure Island?" Kiva asked, her eyebrows raised.

Ora nodded. "Yeah, we can use the big tree as the treasure spot, and the goal of the game is to work together to find clues hidden around the playground. Each person has a job to do. Some people can look for clues, some can solve puzzles, and others can protect the treasure from being taken. It's all about teamwork, and everyone has an important role, even if they can't run fast or climb the tree."

Her friends exchanged excited looks. It was a brilliant idea, and they could already imagine how much fun it would be.

"Let's do it!" Remi said, pumping her fist into the air.

The next day, they arrived at the playground with a plan. They spent part of the morning making simple "clues" out of paper and hiding them in various spots around the playground—some near the swings, others by the big tree, and even one near the quiet corner where Sami often stood. They also wrote out a few puzzles and riddles that the children would need to solve to find the treasure.

When recess came, Ora and her friends gathered at the big tree and started inviting kids to join the game.

"Hey, Sami!" Ora called as she saw him standing by the edge of the soccer field, watching but never playing. "We're going to play a new game called Treasure Island. Do you want to play with us?"

Sami looked uncertain, but the kindness in Ora's voice made him feel safe. He took a few steps toward the group, glancing around nervously. "What do I have to do?" he asked quietly.

Ora smiled. "You'll help solve the puzzles and protect the treasure. We need you to be the keeper of the clues."

Sami's face lit up a little. "Okay. I'll try."

Next, Ora approached Althea, who was sitting by herself near the edge of the playground in her wheelchair. "Althea, we're playing Treasure Island, and I thought you might like to join us. You can be the one who solves the hardest puzzles, the ones no one else can figure out."

Althea looked surprised but pleased. "Really? I can help?"

"Of course," Ora said. "We need you."

One by one, more kids began to join the game. Some of them were the fast runners, like the kids from the Big Slide, but others were like Sami and Althea—children who had never really been invited to play before. Ora explained the rules, making sure that everyone understood their role and knew that every job was important.

As the game began, something magical happened. Sami, usually so quiet and withdrawn, took charge of the clues, guiding the other children as they searched for pieces of the treasure map. Althea used her sharp mind to solve the most difficult riddles, impressing everyone with how quickly she figured them out.

The children worked together, running around the playground, laughing and helping one another. For the first time, no one was left out. No one was sitting on the sidelines, watching but not participating.

When the final clue was solved, and the "treasure" (a pile of colorful marbles Ora had brought from home) was found under the big tree, everyone cheered. The game had been a huge success. Even the kids who had been hesitant at first were now smiling, having had a great time.

7 Lessons Learned from Chapter 1

1. **Inclusivity is intentional**: Creating an environment where everyone feels welcome requires planning and effort.
2. **Teamwork makes a difference**: When people work together, everyone's unique skills can shine.
3. **Everyone has value**: No matter what someone's abilities are, they can contribute to the group in meaningful ways.
4. **Breaking down barriers creates joy**: When kids from different groups play together, they discover how fun it is to include everyone.
5. **Creativity can solve problems**: Inventing new games and rules can open up opportunities for more people to participate.
6. **Small actions lead to big changes**: Starting with a simple game can be the first step toward making lasting changes in a community.
7. **Kindness encourages bravery**: When someone feels safe and included, they are more likely to step out of their comfort zone and join in.

Chapter 2: The Spark of Change

The next day, Ora, Remi, Kiva, and Dano could feel the excitement as they walked toward the playground. Yesterday's game of *Treasure Island* had been a huge success. Sami and Althea had both joined in, and for the first time, they hadn't been left out. The other kids had enjoyed themselves, too, and Ora couldn't wait to see what they could come up with next.

But there was still work to be done. As they stepped out onto the blacktop and looked around, they saw that not everyone had caught the spirit of change. Some kids were still playing in their usual groups. The children on the soccer field kicked the ball back and forth like they always did, and the group around the Big Slide raced to see who could slide the fastest. Meanwhile, Althea sat near the swings again, and Sami stood off to the side, hesitant to join the games unless someone specifically invited him.

Ora felt a small tug of disappointment. "It was fun yesterday," she said to her friends as they headed toward the big tree, "but it feels like not everyone understands that the playground can be different now. We still have work to do."

Dano nodded. "We made a good start with *Treasure Island,* but we need to think bigger."

Remi was already on board. "Yeah, we need a new game—something that'll make *everyone* want to join in. Even the kids who don't usually play."

Kiva glanced over at the soccer field, where a few kids from the older grades were showing off their skills. "It's tricky. Some of the kids like doing their own thing. How do we make them want to play something new?"

Ora thought about it. The idea that had sparked the day before—about making the playground a place where everyone could play—was still burning bright inside her. She just needed to figure out how to keep the flame going.

"Well," she said slowly, "what if we make something that isn't just a game, but a whole adventure? A game where everyone gets to be a hero, no matter what they're good at."

Her friends looked intrigued, so Ora explained. "We could create a game where the playground turns into a whole new world. We could have different zones, just like in a real adventure—like a forest, a cave, or even a magic castle! Every player could choose a different role, depending on what they like to do. Some kids could be explorers, others could solve puzzles or figure out secret codes. And the best part is, we make sure that every zone is easy for everyone to access."

"That sounds amazing!" Kiva said, her eyes wide with excitement. "But how would we do it? We can't exactly build a castle."

"We don't need to," Ora replied, smiling. "We can use our imaginations! And we can use things already on the playground. Like, the jungle gym could be the castle, and the big tree could be the forest. We could make it an adventure where everyone has a part to play."

Remi grinned. "I love it! And we could create special challenges in each zone, so every kid can have a chance to help the team win."

Dano, always the thinker of the group, was already planning the logistics. "We'll need to make sure that the challenges aren't just for the fastest or the strongest kids. Maybe some challenges can be about thinking, or working together to solve a problem."

"Exactly," Ora agreed. "That way, even kids like Althea or Sami can have a big role in the game."

The more they talked, the more the plan took shape. They decided to call the game *Adventure Quest*. There would be three main zones—the Forest (the area around the big tree), the Castle (the jungle gym), and the River (the line of swings). Each player would get to choose a role in the adventure: they could be an explorer, a puzzle solver, a protector, or a helper. Every role was important, and the adventure wouldn't succeed unless everyone worked together.

By the time recess rolled around, Ora and her friends had everything ready. They had drawn out maps of the playground-turned-adventure-land, with instructions for each zone. They even came up with simple puzzles and challenges that the players could complete to move from one zone to the next.

As soon as the recess bell rang, Ora and her friends rushed outside, eager to get started. They went straight to the big tree and began setting up the game. Kiva and Dano spread out to tell the other kids about *Adventure Quest,* inviting everyone to join. Remi drew a large, imaginary map in the dirt to show where each zone was located.

At first, only a few kids came over, curious about what was going on. But once Ora explained the adventure to them, they were hooked.

"So, it's like we're going on a quest?" asked a boy named Finn, who usually only played soccer.

"Exactly!" Ora said. "You'll need to work with your team to get through all the zones and complete the adventure. You can be an explorer, or you can help solve the puzzles to move the team forward."

"Can I be a protector?" Sami asked quietly, surprising Ora with his enthusiasm. "I want to help keep everyone safe during the quest."

"Of course!" Ora replied, beaming. "You'll be in charge of making sure the explorers don't get 'lost' in the forest zone."

Sami smiled shyly, clearly excited about his new role. More kids started to gather around as the news of the adventure spread. Even Althea wheeled her chair over to the group.

"What's my job in the adventure?" Althea asked, her eyes shining with anticipation.

"You get to be the puzzle master," Ora said. "Every time the team reaches a challenge, you'll help them figure it out."

Althea's grin was as bright as the sun. "I love solving puzzles! This is going to be so fun!"

Before long, nearly the entire playground had joined *Adventure Quest*. Some kids who usually stuck to their own groups, like those at the Big Slide or on the soccer field, wandered over to see what the fuss was about. Ora welcomed them all with open arms, explaining that every player was important and that the adventure couldn't be completed without everyone's help.

As the game progressed, something magical happened again—just like the day before. The kids who were used to sticking to their own activities started working together. The fast kids helped guide the explorers through the different zones, while the quieter kids used their brains to solve puzzles and find hidden clues. Even the kids who usually didn't talk much, like Sami and Althea, became leaders in their own way.

By the end of recess, the entire playground had been transformed—not just by the game, but by the way the children had come together. They hadn't just completed *Adventure Quest*; they had created a whole new world where everyone had a place, and everyone's abilities were valued.

7 Lessons Learned from Chapter 2:

1. **Creativity can build inclusivity**: Imagination helps create spaces where everyone can participate, regardless of ability.
2. **Adventure brings people together**: Shared experiences help bridge divides between different groups.
3. **Leadership comes in many forms**: Even quiet or reserved individuals can become leaders when given the right role.
4. **Teamwork creates success**: Achieving a common goal requires contributions from everyone, highlighting the importance of collaboration.
5. **Kindness inspires confidence**: Inviting someone to participate can give them the courage to step forward.
6. **Inclusion takes time**: Change doesn't happen overnight, but

small steps can lead to big progress.

7. **Everyone is a hero**: In the right environment, everyone has something special to offer, making them a valuable part of the team.

Chapter 3: The Plan Begins

The day after *Adventure Quest* was another bright, sunny morning at Sunnyhill Elementary. Ora and her friends couldn't wait to continue their mission to make the playground a place where everyone could play. As they gathered by the big tree at recess, they felt excited but also a little uncertain. They had pulled off two great games so far, but if they wanted to truly change the playground for good, they knew they needed a bigger plan.

"We've done *Treasure Island* and *Adventure Quest*," Ora said, leaning against the tree and looking around the playground. "But what happens when we stop organizing games? Will everything go back to the way it was?"

Her friends were quiet for a moment, thinking. Dano was the first to speak. "It's true. Even though the games are fun, the playground is still divided when we're not here organizing things."

Kiva nodded. "Yeah, I've noticed that too. It's like some kids still go back to their old groups after the games are over. We need something that'll keep everyone playing together, even when we're not leading the way."

"I think we need to make permanent changes," Remi suggested, her eyes lighting up with an idea. "What if we redesign the playground itself? Not just the games, but the space too, so everyone feels welcome no matter where they are."

Ora's heart skipped a beat. Redesigning the playground sounded like a huge task—but an exciting one. "That's a great idea, Remi! If the playground is set up to include everyone, kids will naturally play together without needing special games."

"But how do we do that?" Kiva asked, glancing at the swings and the soccer field. "We don't have the power to build things like ramps or new equipment."

"We don't need to start with the big stuff right away," Ora said. "Let's think about what we *can* do. Maybe we can organize the playground differently or create spaces where kids can mix together more easily."

The idea of changing the way the playground was used, rather than the physical structure itself, made the task seem less overwhelming. They could start with small changes, just like they had with the games.

"What about making new spaces?" Dano suggested. "Like, instead of everyone going to the same old spots, we could make new 'zones' that bring different kids together. Maybe we could put up signs or create areas for specific activities that everyone can enjoy."

"That's brilliant!" Remi exclaimed. "And we could use things we already have to make those areas special. Like how we used the tree for *Treasure Island*. We could turn the swings into a part of a bigger game, or make the quiet corner a place for storytelling or puzzle-solving."

Ora's mind was buzzing with possibilities. "What if we also created a buddy system? Each day, kids could team up with someone new, and they'd have to work together to complete activities or challenges. It would give everyone a chance to play with different people."

"I love that idea!" Kiva said, grinning. "It'll help kids who don't usually talk to each other become friends."

The more they talked, the more the plan came together. They decided to divide the playground into different zones where kids could play together in ways that encouraged teamwork, creativity, and inclusion. Here's what they came up with:

- **The Forest Zone**: This would be an area around the big tree, perfect for exploring, scavenger hunts, and imaginative play.
- **The Puzzle Pavilion**: Using the quiet corner, they would create a space for puzzles, riddles, and problem-solving games where everyone could contribute, no matter their ability.
- **The Swing Zone**: They'd create team-based games that

involved the swings, like relay races or challenges that used rhythm and coordination.

- **The Friendship Field**: The soccer field would be transformed into a place for inclusive games where teams mixed up every day, with rules that made sure everyone had a chance to participate, even if they weren't the fastest or strongest.

After school, they decided to meet in Ora's backyard to make a real plan. Ora's mom had already set up a picnic table for them, knowing the group often gathered for their creative brainstorming sessions. As they sat together with notebooks and markers, they started drawing out their ideas, sketching maps of the playground and listing different activities they could organize.

The Forest Zone was Kiva's project. "We could hide things around the tree every morning," she said, excitedly scribbling notes. "Kids would have to work together to find clues or solve puzzles that take them from one part of the playground to another."

Dano was in charge of the Puzzle Pavilion. "I'll come up with different brain teasers every week," he said, drawing a diagram of the quiet corner. "The puzzles will have different levels, so there'll be something for everyone—easy ones for the younger kids and harder ones for the older ones. Althea will love this."

Remi, who was great with organizing games, took charge of the Swing Zone. "We can make up new games every week," she said, tapping her pen against her chin as she thought. "We'll create challenges that use the swings in fun ways—like a timed obstacle course where one team has to swing in rhythm while the other completes a task."

Ora was in charge of the Friendship Field. "We'll make sure the teams change every day so no one gets left out. I'll think of games where teamwork is more important than speed or skill. Maybe we could even get the teachers to help referee, so everyone gets a fair chance."

As they finalized their plan, they realized they needed a way to explain the new playground zones to the other kids. They couldn't just change things overnight without letting everyone know what was happening.

"We need to make an announcement," Ora said, "but it has to be fun, not like a boring speech."

Remi's face lit up. "What if we make posters and hang them around the school? We could draw pictures of the zones and explain the new games. That way, everyone will see it and get excited!"

"And we could even make a mini presentation during lunch," Kiva added. "Just a quick thing to tell everyone what we're doing."

Ora loved the idea. "Let's do both. We'll spend the rest of the week getting everything ready, and by next Monday, we'll launch the new playground plan!"

The next few days were a blur of activity. After school, Ora and her friends worked hard on making colorful posters with catchy slogans like "Join the Fun in the Forest Zone!" and "The Puzzle Pavilion Needs You!" They drew pictures of the big tree, the swings, and the soccer field, turning each space into a place of adventure and inclusion.

On Friday, they asked the principal if they could make a short announcement during lunch. The principal, who had noticed the positive changes happening on the playground, was happy to let them share their plan.

When Monday morning finally arrived, Ora and her friends were ready. The posters were hanging all over the school, and excitement buzzed in the air. At lunch, Ora stood in front of her classmates, feeling a bit nervous but mostly excited.

"Hey, everyone!" she said, her voice bright and cheerful. "You've probably noticed the posters around school. My friends and I are working on something special for the playground. We're creating new zones where everyone can play, no matter what they like to do. There's something for everyone—puzzles, adventures, teamwork games—and we want you all to join in!"

Kiva, Remi, and Dano each took turns explaining the zones they were in charge of, and by the time they were finished, the cafeteria was buzzing with excitement. Kids were talking about which zone they wanted to explore first, and many of them couldn't wait to try out the new games.

7 Lessons Learned from Chapter 3:

1. **Change starts with a plan**: Big ideas are more likely to succeed when you break them down into smaller, manageable steps.
2. **Everyone can contribute**: By dividing responsibilities, each person can use their unique talents to help a bigger cause.
3. **Imagination is powerful**: Creativity can turn ordinary spaces into places of adventure and inclusion.
4. **Inclusivity requires effort**: Making sure everyone feels welcome takes planning and persistence.
5. **Leadership means involving others**: True leaders encourage others to take part and share ownership of the project.
6. **Communication is key**: To get people excited about a new idea, you need to explain it clearly and in a fun way.
7. **Teamwork brings big changes**: Working together makes it easier to create lasting change.

Chapter 4: Meeting New Friends

The buzz from the playground changes spread quickly through Sunnyhill Elementary. Word had gotten around about Ora's plan to create new zones where everyone could play, and many kids were excited to see what the new week would bring. Some were already talking about which zone they'd visit first—whether it would be the Forest Zone with its hidden treasures, the Puzzle Pavilion for solving challenges, the Swing Zone with its rhythmic games, or the Friendship Field where teamwork was key.

But Ora knew there were still kids who might feel unsure about joining in. Not everyone was as quick to jump into something new, especially if they hadn't always felt included before. Ora's goal wasn't just to create new spaces; she wanted to make sure that every single kid felt like the playground was their place, too.

As she and her friends stood by the big tree that Monday morning, Ora scanned the playground for those kids who might need a little extra encouragement. Her eyes soon fell on Althea, who was wheeling herself toward the school entrance. Althea hadn't been to the playground yet that day, but Ora remembered how much fun she'd had during *Treasure Island* and *Adventure Quest*. Althea had loved solving puzzles and working with the group, but she didn't always feel comfortable coming to the playground on her own.

Ora waved to her. "Althea! Come join us!"

Althea turned her chair in their direction and smiled. "Hey, Ora! What's happening today?"

"We've got something new going on," Ora explained, excited. "We've created different zones for everyone to play in, and I thought you'd love the Puzzle Pavilion. It's going to be a spot where we can solve challenges together."

Althea's face lit up. "That sounds awesome! What kinds of puzzles are we solving?"

Ora grinned. "Dano's in charge of the Puzzle Pavilion, and he's got all sorts of ideas. There's a riddle challenge, a memory game, and even some problem-solving tasks where you'll need to work with others to crack codes."

"Count me in!" Althea said eagerly, wheeling her chair closer. "I can't wait to try it."

Ora's heart lifted. That was one more friend who felt included, but she wasn't done yet. As the other kids started to spread out to different zones, Ora spotted Sami, standing off to the side of the playground near the soccer field. He had joined in before, but Ora knew he was still shy and sometimes unsure of himself. He always looked like he wanted to join in, but something held him back.

Ora walked over to him. "Hey, Sami! You've gotta see what we're doing today. You'd be great in the Friendship Field."

Sami glanced at the soccer field, where a group of older kids were already running drills, and shook his head. "I'm not good at soccer."

"It's not just soccer," Ora said quickly. "The Friendship Field isn't about being the fastest or the best player. It's about working together, making sure everyone has fun. We're playing a new game today where everyone gets a role, and I know you'll be great at it."

Sami looked down, shuffling his feet. "What if I mess up?"

"You won't mess up," Ora said gently. "And even if you do, that's okay! The whole point is to try together, to help each other out. No one has to do it all on their own."

Sami hesitated, but there was something in Ora's warm smile that made him feel safe. Slowly, he nodded. "Okay. I'll give it a try."

Ora beamed. "Awesome! You're going to do great."

As Sami and Althea headed toward their zones, Ora felt hopeful. But there was one more person she had in mind. She spotted her at the edge of the playground, sitting alone on a bench. Her name was Laria, a new girl at the school. Ora had noticed her around before, but Laria always seemed distant, keeping to herself during recess.

Ora had never spoken to Laria much, but now seemed like the perfect time to change that. She walked over to the bench and sat down next to her.

"Hi, Laria," Ora said softly. "How are you?"

Laria looked up, surprised that someone had approached her. "I'm fine," she said quietly, her eyes darting back down to her shoes.

Ora could sense Laria's discomfort, but she pressed on gently. "I've seen you sitting here a lot during recess. Have you ever thought about joining in on the games?"

Laria shrugged. "I don't really know anyone yet. It's hard to just...jump in."

Ora nodded, understanding. "I get that. But you know what? We've been working on something new. We've set up zones all over the playground where kids can play together, and we'd love for you to join us. You don't have to know anyone yet; you'll meet people while you're playing. It's all about having fun and making friends."

Laria glanced up, a small flicker of curiosity in her eyes. "What kind of games?"

Ora smiled. "There's a lot to choose from. You could explore the Forest Zone and go on a treasure hunt, solve puzzles in the Puzzle Pavilion, or work with a team in the Friendship Field. There's something for everyone."

For the first time, Laria seemed to consider it. "Maybe I could try the Forest Zone," she said softly. "I like the idea of exploring."

Ora grinned. "That's a great choice. I'll walk you over there and introduce you to the others."

As the two of them made their way to the Forest Zone, Ora felt a sense of accomplishment. She had always believed that the playground should be a place where *everyone* could feel comfortable and included, and now it was starting to happen. One by one, the kids who had once felt left out were joining in, finding their place in the new playground.

When they reached the Forest Zone, Kiva was already there, setting up for the first adventure of the day. She smiled when she saw Ora and Laria approaching. "Hey, Ora! Who's this?"

"This is Laria," Ora said, placing a friendly hand on Laria's shoulder. "She's new to the school, and I thought she'd love to join in on the treasure hunt."

Kiva's face lit up. "Welcome, Laria! You're just in time. We're about to start searching for hidden treasure. We've got clues hidden all around the playground, and we need explorers to help us find them."

Laria smiled shyly. "That sounds fun."

As Laria joined the group of kids in the Forest Zone, Ora felt a sense of pride swell in her chest. The new zones were working—kids who had never played together before were mixing, making new friends, and having fun. The playground wasn't just a place for games anymore; it was becoming a place for connection, for growth, and for inclusivity.

7 Lessons Learned from Chapter 4:

1. **Inclusivity often requires a personal invitation**: Some people need encouragement to join in, especially if they've felt left out before.
2. **Kindness builds confidence**: A simple gesture of inclusion can help others find the courage to participate.
3. **Diversity in activities helps everyone feel included**: Offering different types of games and zones means there's something for everyone.
4. **Friendships grow when we reach out**: Taking the time to get to know someone new can open the door to new connections.
5. **Patience is important when building community**: Not everyone will join in right away, but with gentle encouragement, most will eventually feel comfortable.

6. **Small steps can lead to big changes**: Introducing new games and spaces can gradually transform an entire environment.

7. **Leadership means thinking of others**: True leaders make sure that no one is left behind, and they work to create spaces where everyone feels valued.

Chapter 5: Designing Games for Everyone

The next morning, Ora and her friends arrived early at school. The excitement from yesterday's successful introduction of the playground zones was still fresh in their minds, but they knew there was more work to be done. They gathered at their usual spot beneath the big tree, ready to take on their next challenge—designing even more games that would include *everyone*, especially those who might still feel left out.

"I feel like yesterday was a big win," Dano said, glancing around at the still-empty playground. "But I noticed there are still some kids who didn't really join in. It's like they were curious but unsure about getting involved."

"Yeah," Kiva agreed, picking at the grass by her feet. "We've made some progress, but we need to figure out how to make the zones and games even more inviting. Maybe some kids are nervous about not being good at a particular game, like sports or puzzles."

Ora nodded thoughtfully. "Not everyone is fast, and not everyone likes solving puzzles. That's okay, though. It just means we need to create even more variety—different kinds of games that don't depend on being good at one thing. Something that's just fun."

Remi chimed in, her eyes lighting up with excitement. "What if we make up some new games where the rules are flexible? Games that can be played in different ways depending on who's playing."

"That's a great idea!" Ora said. "If the rules can change to fit the players, no one will feel like they don't belong. It'll give everyone a chance to enjoy the game, no matter what they're good at."

Dano scratched his head thoughtfully. "How do we start? We already have some cool zones, but we need new games that make use of everything. Maybe something with a mix of running, thinking, and teamwork."

As they brainstormed, ideas began to flow. They knew they had to create games that were as varied as the kids on the playground, so they started by listing some activities that different kids would enjoy:

- **Running and Adventure**: For kids who loved to run and explore, they wanted to create a fast-paced adventure game that didn't rely on just speed, but also quick thinking and problem-solving.
- **Creative Problem Solving**: For kids like Althea who enjoyed puzzles, they planned to integrate challenges that required teamwork to solve, but without needing to run or be physically active.
- **Strategy and Planning**: Some kids preferred strategy-based games where they could use their brains instead of their bodies, so they needed to come up with games where strategy was the key to winning.
- **Inclusive Movement**: They also wanted to design games that included everyone, regardless of their physical abilities, so kids like Althea or those who might not be able to run fast could still participate fully.

Once they had these broad categories, the ideas started to take shape.

The Magic Map was their first new idea. It was a game that took place across the entire playground, using the different zones like a giant board game. Each zone represented a different part of a magical kingdom—The Forest Zone could be the Enchanted Woods, the Swing Zone could be the Cloud Mountains, and so on.

The goal was for the players to work together to find hidden "map pieces" scattered throughout the zones. Each map piece contained a clue or a riddle, and the players had to solve these to reveal the next part of the kingdom. The twist was that each player had a unique role based on what they liked to do. Runners could be the "Seekers," searching for the hidden map pieces. The puzzle-lovers, like Althea, could be the "Decoders," solving the clues that revealed the next location. And kids who enjoyed strategy could be the "Planners," making decisions about which zone to visit next.

The best part? No one was left out, and everyone's contribution was vital to completing the map.

After *The Magic Map* idea was solidified, they came up with another game called **Rhythm Relay.** This game took place mainly in the Swing Zone, but could be adapted for other areas too. In this game, teams of players had to pass an imaginary baton through rhythmic movements. The twist was that not all the movements had to involve running. One part of the relay could involve using the swings in rhythm, while another part might require solving a riddle or working together to create a pattern of claps or steps.

"Rhythm Relay sounds perfect for the Swing Zone," Remi said, sketching out the rules on a piece of paper. "It's all about timing and working together, and it doesn't matter how fast you are. It's more about coordination, and it'll be fun for kids who like music or dancing too."

"I think it could be a hit," Ora said, grinning. "Plus, it's a good way to get everyone moving together without making anyone feel like they have to compete."

Next, they developed **The Story Quest,** an imaginative game that combined creativity with adventure. In this game, the players created a story together as they moved through the playground zones. Each zone had a different part of the story—a beginning, middle, and end. The Forest Zone might be the scene where the characters meet magical creatures, while the Puzzle Pavilion could be where the heroes have to solve a riddle to unlock the next part of the tale. The kids could act out their characters or simply narrate what happens next, letting their imaginations take the lead.

"Story Quest is great for kids who like to use their imaginations," Dano said, excited. "It's not about winning or losing; it's about building a story together. And it's flexible. If someone wants to be a knight, they can be. If someone else wants to be a wizard or a dragon, that's cool too."

Ora loved how the game ideas were coming together. They had games for kids who liked running, for those who preferred thinking, and even for those who loved telling stories. It felt like they were creating something that could truly bring everyone together.

By the time the recess bell rang, they were ready to introduce the new games. They decided to start with *The Magic Map,* since it involved the whole playground and was a good way to get as many kids involved as possible.

As they explained the rules to their classmates, there was an eager energy in the air. The idea of the playground turning into a magical kingdom with hidden map pieces sparked excitement. Kids who usually stuck to their own groups began to team up, excited to take on the different roles of Seekers, Decoders, and Planners.

Sami was one of the first to step forward, volunteering to be a Seeker. He had grown more confident since joining the Friendship Field games, and Ora was thrilled to see him getting involved so quickly.

Althea, as expected, chose to be a Decoder. She loved solving puzzles, and the idea of working together to reveal hidden clues excited her.

As the game began, kids ran to different zones, looking for the hidden map pieces that Ora and her friends had carefully placed earlier that morning. The runners darted around, while the Decoders waited for them to return with the clues. Then, they worked together to solve each riddle, figuring out the next location in the magical kingdom.

7 Lessons Learned from Chapter 5:

1. **Games can be flexible**: By designing games with adaptable rules, we can make sure everyone can play, regardless of ability or preference.
2. **Variety keeps things inclusive**: Offering a range of different types of games ensures that there's something for everyone to enjoy.
3. **Collaboration is key**: Games that require teamwork and different skills help bring kids together and value everyone's contributions.
4. **Inclusion creates confidence**: When kids are given roles that suit their strengths, they feel more confident and willing to participate.
5. **Creativity leads to fun**: Imaginative games, like *The Magic Map* and *Story Quest,* show that fun isn't limited to physical abilities.
6. **Everyone has a role to play**: Whether someone is fast, thoughtful, creative, or strategic, there's a place for them in a well-designed game.
7. **Building a sense of community takes time**: Each new game and activity brought the kids closer, transforming the playground into a more inclusive space.

Chapter 6: The First Game

The morning after *The Magic Map* was introduced, there was a buzz of excitement at Sunnyhill Elementary. Word had spread quickly about the fun and inclusive game that Ora and her friends had created, and now kids who had sat out the day before were eager to join in. As Ora and her friends stood by the big tree, preparing for another day of play, they were thrilled to see even more kids gathering around, excited for the next game.

But with the new excitement came new challenges. Ora could see that some of the kids weren't entirely sure about joining in, especially those who weren't used to playing in groups or participating in games that required teamwork. Some were hesitant, unsure of what role they would play or if they'd be good enough to help their team. Others were still sticking to their old groups, waiting to see if this new playground dynamic would last.

Ora knew that today's game had to be just as inclusive as *The Magic Map,* but perhaps a little simpler so that everyone, even those feeling unsure, would be able to jump right in without feeling overwhelmed.

Remi had an idea. "What if we play *Treasure Island* again today?" she suggested as they gathered their friends. "It was fun when we first played it, and it's easy for everyone to understand. Plus, it's not too competitive. That way, the new kids who want to play can get involved without feeling pressured."

"I like it," Ora said, nodding. "It's a good balance. We can still use the zones, but keep the game easy and fun."

Dano agreed. "And we can give everyone specific roles, like last time, so no one feels left out. We'll make sure every role is important."

The plan was set. They would bring back *Treasure Island,* but with a few new twists to make it even more inclusive and exciting. The idea was simple: the entire playground would be the "island," and the kids would be divided into small teams, each working together to find hidden treasures scattered across different zones. There would be clues to follow, but instead of racing to be the fastest, the goal was to complete challenges and solve puzzles as a team.

Each team needed a mix of skills—some kids to explore and find clues, others to solve puzzles, and a few to be "protectors" who would make sure the treasure wasn't "stolen" by other teams. The best part was that the game could be adapted depending on how each team worked together. If one team had kids who weren't fast runners, they could rely more on puzzle-solving or strategy.

As soon as recess began, Ora and her friends set up the game. They scattered clues around the playground zones and hid the treasures—small, colorful tokens that Ora had made at home—inside secret spots, like under the big tree or near the swings.

By the time they were ready, a large group of kids had gathered. Ora looked around, excited to see so many different faces—kids from the soccer field, kids from the quiet corner, and even some of the older kids who usually didn't join in playground games.

"Welcome to *Treasure Island*!" Ora announced, smiling at the eager crowd. "We've got hidden treasures all over the playground, and it's your job to find them! You'll be working in teams, and each team needs a mix of explorers, puzzle solvers, and protectors. The goal isn't to be the fastest, but to work together and make sure your team finds as many treasures as possible."

The kids buzzed with excitement as they broke into teams. Ora made sure to assign roles to everyone, encouraging the quieter kids, like Sami, to take on leadership positions. Sami, who had grown more confident over the past few days, volunteered to be a protector, guarding his team's treasure and helping with clues.

Althea, in her wheelchair, was thrilled to be a puzzle solver again. She had brought along a notebook and pencil, ready to jot down clues and riddles. She had loved the role during *The Magic Map* and was eager to show off her skills once more.

Remi and Dano went from team to team, helping to explain the rules and making sure everyone felt comfortable with their roles. Even Laria, the new girl who had been hesitant at first, joined a team of explorers. Ora smiled when she saw Laria excitedly talking with her teammates, already looking more comfortable than she had just a few days ago.

As the game began, the playground transformed into an island of adventure. Teams spread out across the zones, searching for hidden clues and solving puzzles. Some kids ran to the Forest Zone, where they searched around the big tree for hidden treasures, while others stayed closer to the swings, working on solving a tricky riddle that would lead them to the next location.

Ora watched proudly as the teams worked together. There were no arguments about who was fastest or who was the best at solving puzzles. Everyone had an important role, and the game required each team to communicate and collaborate. It wasn't just about finding the treasures; it was about how well the kids could work together to solve problems and complete the challenges.

At one point, Sami's team found themselves stuck on a particularly hard clue hidden near the Puzzle Pavilion. They had found the token, but the riddle attached to it was difficult, and none of the kids seemed to know the answer.

Sami, who was usually shy, spoke up. "Maybe we're thinking about it wrong," he suggested. "What if the answer isn't about the playground, but about something we've already seen?"

The other kids on his team listened, nodding thoughtfully.

"That's a great idea!" said one of the older kids. "Let's go back and check the first clue again."

Sami smiled shyly as the team followed his suggestion, and sure enough, they found the answer to the riddle. It was a small moment, but it was a big deal for Sami, who had always been more of an observer than a leader. Ora beamed when she saw him growing into his role.

Meanwhile, in the Forest Zone, Althea was hard at work solving another puzzle with her team. The clue was written in a secret code, and it was up to her to figure out what it meant. She scribbled notes in her notebook, breaking the code piece by piece while her teammates cheered her on.

"I've got it!" Althea announced triumphantly after a few minutes. "The treasure is hidden near the jungle gym!"

Her team raced off to claim their prize, with Althea leading the way in her wheelchair. For the first time in a long time, she felt like she was an essential part of the team.

As the game continued, the playground was filled with laughter, shouts of joy, and the excited chatter of kids working together. There were no arguments or kids feeling left out; everyone was having fun, and everyone's contributions were valued.

By the end of recess, all the treasures had been found, and the teams gathered around the big tree to celebrate their success. Ora and her friends handed out small prizes—stickers and colorful bracelets—to everyone who had participated.

"You all did amazing today!" Ora said, smiling at the tired but happy group. "It wasn't about who found the most treasures; it was about how well you worked together. That's what makes this playground special—everyone gets to be part of the fun."

7 Lessons Learned from Chapter 6:

1. **Teamwork is key**: Games that emphasize collaboration over competition help build friendships and make sure everyone feels included.
2. **Everyone has a role to play**: When kids are given specific roles based on their strengths, they feel more confident and valued.
3. **Leadership can come from unexpected places**: Even quieter kids, like Sami, can become leaders when given the right

opportunity.

4. **Inclusivity is about flexibility**: Designing games that allow for different abilities and skills helps ensure that no one is left out.

5. **Communication is important**: Working together requires good communication, and games like *Treasure Island* encourage kids to share ideas and listen to each other.

6. **Success is measured in participation, not winning**: The real victory is when everyone has fun and feels like they belong.

7. **Inclusivity takes ongoing effort**: Building a welcoming environment doesn't happen overnight—it's something that needs to be nurtured and developed over time.

Chapter 7: Facing Resistance

Despite the success of the new playground games like *Treasure Island* and *The Magic Map,* Ora and her friends soon realized that not everyone was on board with the changes. While most of the kids were excited to join in the new games, there were still a few who resisted the idea of playing together with kids they didn't know or who weren't like them.

It started the next morning, just as the bell rang for recess. Ora, Remi, Kiva, and Dano had planned to run *Rhythm Relay* in the Swing Zone, a game they'd designed to encourage teamwork and coordination. They were excited to introduce the game to the other kids, but when they arrived at the swings, they found a group of older boys already there, hogging all the swings.

Finn, one of the boys who had sometimes joined in their games, was leading the group. He was swinging high, laughing with his friends as they competed to see who could swing the fastest and jump the farthest. Ora approached them cautiously, hoping to explain the new game.

"Hey, Finn!" she called out cheerfully. "We're setting up a new game today—*Rhythm Relay*—and we need the swings for part of it. Do you and your friends want to join in?"

Finn slowed his swing but didn't get off. He gave Ora a doubtful look. "What's *Rhythm Relay*?"

Ora explained, her voice bright and enthusiastic. "It's a team game where we have to work together to pass a rhythm down the line using swings, clapping, and movement. It's really fun, and everyone gets a chance to play!"

But Finn didn't look convinced. "Sounds boring. We were about to see who could jump the farthest off the swings," he said, smirking at his friends. "I don't think we need any new games."

Ora felt her heart sink a little. She had hoped that after all the success of the past few days, everyone would want to participate in the new inclusive games. But Finn and his friends weren't interested in teamwork; they were focused on competing and showing off.

"Come on," Ora said, trying again. "It's not about jumping the farthest—it's about working together. Plus, there's still plenty of time to use the swings for fun later."

Finn hopped off his swing and crossed his arms. "We don't need to work together. We're having fun already. Why should we change just because you say so?"

Some of the other kids standing nearby started to whisper, and Ora felt a flush of embarrassment rise to her cheeks. She wasn't trying to force anyone to do anything, but she also knew that the playground couldn't truly be a place for everyone if some kids insisted on keeping things exclusive.

Remi stepped forward, sensing Ora's discomfort. "It's not about changing everything," she said calmly. "We're just trying to make sure everyone gets a chance to play. If you don't want to join the game, that's okay, but we need the swings for this round."

Finn rolled his eyes. "You guys can play your games, but we're going to keep doing our own thing."

With that, he turned and led his friends away from the swings, but not before casting a look back at Ora and muttering, "This is why things were fine before. Not everyone wants to play with everyone."

As they walked off, Ora felt a pang of frustration. Finn's words stung more than she cared to admit. She had worked so hard to make the playground a place for everyone, and it hurt to see some kids resisting that change.

"Don't let him get to you," Kiva said gently, resting a hand on Ora's shoulder. "Some people just don't like things being different."

"But it's not just about being different," Ora said quietly. "It's about making things fair. I just wish they could see that."

Remi sighed. "I know. But not everyone's going to understand right away. We're changing something that's been the same for a long time. It's going to take time."

Ora nodded, though her heart still felt heavy. She glanced around the playground and noticed a few other kids watching the exchange, clearly unsure of what to do. Some of them looked hesitant to join the game now, as if Finn's words had cast doubt over the whole idea.

"We can't give up," Dano said firmly, his voice breaking through Ora's thoughts. "Just because some people don't like change doesn't mean we stop trying. Most of the kids want to play with us. That's what matters."

Ora took a deep breath. Dano was right. They had made a lot of progress, and they couldn't let one setback stop them. If they wanted to make the playground a place where everyone felt welcome, they had to keep going, even when it was hard.

"Okay," Ora said, feeling a bit more determined. "Let's start the game."

As they explained the rules of *Rhythm Relay* to the rest of the kids, Ora could see that many of them were still excited to play. Sami, Althea, Laria, and several other kids eagerly took their positions, ready to try the new game.

The game started smoothly. Kids swung in rhythm, clapping their hands and passing the "baton" through coordinated movements. Laughter filled the air as they worked together to keep the rhythm going. Ora felt her spirits lift as she watched them play, knowing that even though some kids resisted, there were still plenty who believed in what they were doing.

But as the game went on, Ora noticed something else—Finn and his friends had come back, but instead of joining in, they stood off to the side, making jokes and whispering to each other. Occasionally, they would laugh loudly, as if mocking the game.

Ora tried to ignore them, but she couldn't shake the feeling of frustration building inside her. She didn't want to be the kind of person who forced others to do something they didn't want to do, but she also knew that their resistance was having an impact on the other kids. Some of the younger ones kept glancing at Finn's group, clearly unsure whether they should be having fun or feeling self-conscious.

As the game wrapped up and the bell rang for the end of recess, Ora gathered her friends to talk about what had happened.

"I don't get it," Ora said, her brow furrowed. "Why can't Finn and his friends just let us play in peace? They don't have to join us, but it feels like they're trying to make us feel bad for including everyone."

Kiva nodded. "It's like they don't want things to change, and they think making fun of us will stop it from happening."

"I don't think they're bad kids," Remi said thoughtfully. "But I think they're used to things being their way. For a long time, the playground was divided into groups, and they liked it that way because they were in control. Now that things are changing, they're afraid they're losing that control."

Ora frowned. "But this isn't about control. It's about fairness. Everyone should get to play, not just them."

Dano crossed his arms. "Well, it looks like they don't see it that way."

"Maybe," Kiva added, "we need to find a way to get them on board, without making them feel like they're being forced. We can't change their minds by arguing with them, but maybe if they see how much fun everyone else is having, they'll want to join in."

Ora thought about it. Kiva was right. Finn and his friends didn't respond well to being told what to do. They needed to see for themselves that the new games were fun, and that including everyone didn't mean they had to stop having their own fun, too.

7 Lessons Learned from Chapter 7:

1. **Not everyone will embrace change immediately**: Resistance to change is natural, especially when people feel like they're losing control over something familiar.
2. **Fairness isn't always obvious to everyone**: Even when trying to make things fairer, some people may not see the benefits right away.
3. **Mocking or resisting doesn't mean others are right**: Just because someone makes fun of an idea doesn't mean it's a bad one.
4. **Patience is key when dealing with resistance**: Changing minds takes time, and pushing too hard can make things worse.
5. **Leading by example can win people over**: Sometimes the best way to get others on board is to show them the joy and success of inclusion, without forcing them.
6. **Different perspectives come from different experiences**: Kids like Finn might resist because they've benefited from the old system, and change can feel threatening to them.
7. **Perseverance in the face of setbacks is crucial**: One setback shouldn't stop progress—continuing with the plan will eventually bring more people together.

Chapter 8: An Unexpected Ally

The next day, Ora arrived at school with a mix of excitement and apprehension. She knew that the new games were bringing a lot of kids together, but Finn and his friends' resistance was still weighing on her. She didn't want to confront them or force them to play, but their attitude was having an impact. Some of the younger kids seemed nervous about joining in because they didn't want to be teased or left out of what the older, more popular kids were doing.

As Ora and her friends gathered under the big tree to plan that day's activities, Finn's words from the day before echoed in her mind: "This is why things were fine before. Not everyone wants to play with everyone."

But Ora couldn't give up. She knew the playground could be a place where everyone was welcome, and she was determined to find a way to make that happen. Her friends shared her determination, but they, too, seemed a bit unsure of how to handle the resistance.

"We can't just keep pretending Finn and his friends aren't a problem," Remi said, glancing over to where Finn's group was gathering near the soccer field. "They're not playing the games, and they're making the other kids nervous."

"Yeah, it feels like they're pulling kids away from what we're doing," Dano added. "I noticed yesterday that a few of the kids who wanted to play with us were hesitant when they saw Finn and the others hanging around."

Kiva, who had been quiet, spoke up. "Maybe we're going about this the wrong way. What if instead of just ignoring Finn and his group, we tried to get them involved, even in a small way?"

Ora frowned. "I've tried asking them before, but Finn just isn't interested. He thinks our games are boring because they aren't about winning or being the best."

"Maybe we need to show him that our games aren't about winning in the same way, but they're still fun," Kiva suggested. "If we can get just one of them to join us—even for a little while—it might make a difference."

Ora wasn't entirely sure it would work, but she agreed it was worth trying. "Okay," she said. "Let's see if we can get them involved, but we won't push too hard. If they want to stick with their old ways, that's fine. But maybe we can show them that there's more fun to be had when everyone plays together."

As they finalized their plan, Finn's group continued their usual routine of hanging out by the soccer field, kicking the ball back and forth and talking among themselves. It wasn't long before they noticed Ora and her friends setting up for another game. This time, they were preparing to play *Rhythm Relay* again, but they added a twist: the swings would only be part of the game. Other zones would be involved too, so that kids could switch between different roles, like clapping in rhythm, swinging, or solving quick puzzles.

Just as they were about to start explaining the game to the other kids, something unexpected happened.

"Hey, what's going on here?"

Ora turned and saw Vex, one of Finn's closest friends, walking toward the group. Vex was known for being just as competitive as Finn, if not more so, and he usually stuck to the games that involved running, jumping, or showing off some physical skill. But today, there was a curious expression on his face.

"We're about to play *Rhythm Relay*," Ora said cautiously. She wasn't sure if Vex was going to mock the game or ask more questions.

"What's that?" Vex asked, his tone surprisingly neutral.

"It's a game where we have to work together to keep a rhythm going," Remi explained. "There are different parts—you can be on the swings, you can clap in time, or you can help solve a puzzle that keeps the rhythm going. It's all about teamwork."

Vex raised an eyebrow. "Teamwork, huh? So, it's not about who's the fastest or who can swing the highest?"

"No," Ora said. "It's about how well the team works together. Everyone has a different role."

Vex paused, considering this for a moment. "Can I try it?"

Ora blinked, surprised. Vex was actually asking to join?

"Of course!" she said, trying to keep the excitement out of her voice. "We can explain the rules, and you can jump right in. Do you want to try the swings first or start with clapping?"

Vex thought for a moment. "I'll try the swings."

As Ora and her friends explained the rules of *Rhythm Relay* to Vex, some of the other kids who had been hanging back seemed to take notice. If Vex, one of the "cooler" kids, was willing to join in, maybe the game wasn't as silly as they had thought.

Finn and a few of the other boys noticed, too, and Ora saw Finn glance over with a puzzled look on his face. He didn't say anything, but it was clear he was wondering why Vex was joining a game he had dismissed as "boring" the day before.

Once the game started, Vex took his place on the swing, following the rhythm as the rest of the kids clapped and passed the imaginary baton down the line. It didn't take long for him to get into it. To everyone's surprise, Vex turned out to be really good at timing his swings just right to match the clapping, and he even started to enjoy it.

"Hey, this is kind of fun," Vex admitted with a grin. "It's like a game of balance and timing."

Ora smiled. "Exactly! It's not about winning or losing; it's about working together."

As the game progressed, more kids joined in, including some of the ones who had been hesitant before. Even Laria, who had been shy when she first joined the group, was smiling and clapping along with the rhythm, clearly enjoying herself.

When the game ended, Vex looked genuinely pleased. He glanced over at Finn, who had been watching from a distance. For a moment, it seemed like Finn might come over and join the next game, but instead, he just turned away and went back to kicking the soccer ball with his other friends.

Still, Ora felt like they had made some progress. Vex had joined in, and the other kids had seen that the game could be fun, even for someone who was usually more competitive. If they could get one of Finn's friends to join, maybe more would follow.

As the bell rang and the kids headed back to class, Vex caught up with Ora.

"You know," he said, "I thought your games were just for the little kids. But they're actually kind of fun. I might try them again tomorrow."

Ora beamed. "We'd love to have you! We're planning a new game for tomorrow, so if you want to help, you're welcome to join."

Vex gave her a small nod before jogging off to catch up with Finn. Ora watched him go, feeling a mixture of hope and determination. If they could get Vex on board, maybe it wouldn't be long before Finn and the others saw the value in what they were doing too.

7 Lessons Learned from Chapter 8:

1. **Unexpected allies can make a big difference**: Sometimes, the people you least expect to join in can become important supporters.
2. **Teamwork doesn't need to be competitive**: Games that focus on working together can appeal to kids who are usually more competitive, too.
3. **Changing one mind can lead to a bigger shift**: Convincing just one person to join can create a ripple effect that brings more people into the group.
4. **It's okay to take small steps**: Changing the playground's

culture won't happen all at once, but small victories build momentum.

5. **Inclusivity benefits everyone**: When kids of all abilities and interests are included, the whole playground becomes a more fun and welcoming place.

6. **Not everyone will change at the same pace**: Some kids, like Finn, may take longer to embrace the new games, and that's okay.

7. **Perseverance pays off**: Ora and her friends didn't give up, and by staying positive and patient, they were able to make progress.

Chapter 9: Fixing the Problem Zones

The day after Vex had unexpectedly joined the game, Ora felt more hopeful. If someone like Vex, who was always seen as part of Finn's competitive, exclusive group, could join in and enjoy the inclusive games, then maybe there was hope for the rest of them too. However, Ora also knew that there were still parts of the playground that felt "off-limits" to certain kids, and that was a big problem.

The most glaring example of this was the Big Slide. This towering structure, with its high ladder and steep slide, was a place where only the boldest kids went. Kids like Finn dominated the space, turning it into their own territory. The problem was, they had made it clear—whether through teasing, dismissive looks, or just being intimidating—that the Big Slide wasn't for everyone. It had become a symbol of exclusivity, and Ora knew that if they didn't find a way to make the Big Slide accessible to more kids, they would never fully succeed in making the playground a place for everyone.

After school, Ora gathered her friends to talk about the issue.

"The Big Slide is still a problem," she said as they sat in her backyard, brainstorming ideas for the next day. "It's like this barrier between kids who feel confident and those who don't. Some kids are too scared to go near it because Finn and his friends have taken it over."

Remi nodded. "I've seen it too. A few kids wanted to try going on the slide the other day, but Finn's group was hogging it, and they ended up just walking away."

"Yeah," Dano added. "And it's not just the slide. The whole area around it feels like a place where only certain kids are allowed."

Kiva leaned forward, her eyes thoughtful. "Maybe we need to find a way to make the Big Slide feel less...exclusive. If we can figure out how to make it a space where everyone feels welcome, Finn and his friends won't have as much control over it."

Ora agreed. "But how do we do that? It's not like we can just tell Finn and his group to stop using it."

"What if we create a game that *includes* the Big Slide but makes it less about who can go down the fastest or climb the highest?" Dano suggested. "If the slide becomes part of a bigger game where everyone can participate, it might change how kids see it."

"I like that idea," Kiva said. "And we can use the same approach we've been using—making sure that every part of the game involves teamwork and different kinds of skills. That way, even kids who are scared of heights or don't want to climb can still be part of the fun."

The group continued brainstorming, coming up with different ways to integrate the Big Slide into a new game that would make it feel more accessible. Eventually, they settled on an idea called **Slide Quest**—a game that used the Big Slide as one part of a larger adventure that spanned the entire playground.

Here's how the game worked:

- The Big Slide would be the "Mountain" in the adventure. One or two kids from each team would go up the slide to retrieve a flag or clue at the top, but the focus wouldn't be on who could go the fastest. Instead, they would need to work together to retrieve the clue and pass it on to the rest of the team.

- Other zones of the playground would represent different parts of the adventure—such as a "river" near the swings, where kids would have to cross using balance, and a "forest" near the big tree, where they would solve puzzles.

- Each team would need to complete challenges in all the zones, and the key to winning wasn't speed, but how well the team worked together, communicated, and supported one another.

The best part was that there were roles for everyone. Even if a kid didn't want to climb the slide, they could take on other tasks, like solving the puzzles in the Forest Zone or helping their teammates cross the imaginary river.

As they prepared to introduce the game the next day, Ora felt excited but also a little nervous. She knew that Finn and his group would likely be at the Big Slide again, and she wasn't sure how they would react to the new game. But she also knew that if they could turn the Big Slide into a space for everyone, it would be a huge step toward making the playground more inclusive.

The next day at recess, Ora and her friends wasted no time setting up the game. They gathered the kids near the swings and explained the rules of *Slide Quest,* making sure everyone knew that the Big Slide was just one part of the adventure, not the main focus.

As they finished explaining the game, Finn and his friends walked over, clearly curious about what was going on.

"What's this?" Finn asked, his tone skeptical.

"We're playing *Slide Quest,*" Ora explained. "It's a team adventure that uses the whole playground, including the Big Slide. Everyone works together to complete the quest."

Finn raised an eyebrow. "So, it's not just about who can go down the slide the fastest?"

"Nope," Ora said. "The slide is just one part of the game. You have to work with your team to get the flag at the top, and then complete other challenges around the playground."

Finn looked like he wasn't entirely sure whether he liked the idea or not, but then Vex, who had joined the inclusive games earlier, spoke up.

"It's actually fun," Vex said. "You get to do different stuff, not just climb the slide. I played yesterday, and it was pretty cool."

Finn glanced at Vex, then at Ora. "Okay," he said after a moment. "We'll try it."

Ora was surprised but pleased. She hadn't expected Finn to agree so quickly, but she was glad to see that Vex's influence was making a difference.

As the game started, Ora and her friends watched carefully to see how the teams would handle the Big Slide. Finn and his group were clearly competitive—they wanted to get the flag at the top as quickly as possible—but they soon realized that speed alone wouldn't win the game. Once they retrieved the flag, they still had to complete the other challenges, which required communication and teamwork.

The real surprise came when a quieter group of kids, led by Sami and Althea, figured out a clever way to tackle the challenges without rushing. While Finn's group was focused on getting to the slide first, Sami's team took their time working together, solving the puzzles, and making sure every teammate had a role to play. When it came time to climb the slide, Althea couldn't go up herself, but Sami helped his teammates by encouraging them and making sure they knew what to do next.

The other teams, watching this unfold, began to understand that *Slide Quest* wasn't about being the fastest or strongest—it was about how well the team worked together.

By the end of recess, it wasn't Finn's team that won the game, but Sami's. They had completed the quest with careful planning, problem-solving, and teamwork. Finn's group, though fast, had struggled with the challenges that required more thought and cooperation.

Finn looked surprised—and maybe a little frustrated—but Vex seemed impressed. "That was actually pretty smart," Vex said to Sami as they gathered back at the big tree. "You guys figured out the puzzles faster than we did."

Sami smiled shyly. "We just worked together. Everyone had a part."

Finn didn't say much, but Ora could see that something had shifted. Even though Finn's group hadn't won, they had participated in the game without taking over the Big Slide, and that alone felt like a victory.

As the bell rang and the kids headed back to class, Ora and her friends gathered to talk about how the game had gone.

7 Lessons Learned from Chapter 9:

1. **Exclusive spaces can be transformed**: By including the Big Slide in a team game, Ora and her friends changed how kids saw that space, making it more welcoming for everyone.
2. **Teamwork beats speed**: In *Slide Quest,* it wasn't the fastest team that won, but the one that communicated and worked together the best.
3. **Inclusivity benefits everyone**: Even kids who usually dominated the Big Slide learned that playing with others can be just as fun as competing to be the best.
4. **Leadership can come from unexpected places**: Sami, once quiet and unsure, helped lead his team to victory by using his strengths and supporting his teammates.
5. **Influence spreads through example**: Vex's decision to play the game helped encourage Finn and the others to join, showing the power of positive influence.
6. **Persistence pays off**: Ora and her friends didn't give up on the Big Slide, and their determination led to a breakthrough in making the playground more inclusive.
7. **Inclusivity takes many forms**: Making sure that everyone can participate, whether by climbing the slide or solving puzzles, creates a more balanced and fun environment for all.

Chapter 10: Building Bridges of Friendship

The day after *Slide Quest* was another victory for inclusivity on the playground. Ora and her friends felt a sense of pride as more and more kids started participating in the games they had designed. But there was still a challenge that Ora couldn't stop thinking about—while some kids, like Sami and Althea, had fully embraced the changes, others still hesitated. These were the kids who stood on the sidelines, watching but never joining in. Ora knew that if they really wanted to make the playground a place for *everyone,* they needed to find a way to include the ones who hadn't felt confident enough to play yet.

After school that day, Ora gathered her friends again in her backyard. They sat around the picnic table, brainstorming ideas for how to bring more kids into the games.

"Yesterday went great with the Big Slide," Ora began. "But I noticed that there are still kids who don't join in at all. They stand around the edges, watching, but they don't participate. I don't think it's because they don't want to—I think they're just not sure how to get involved."

"I saw that too," Kiva agreed. "It's like they're interested but scared to jump in. Maybe they think they won't be good at the games or that they'll mess up."

Remi nodded. "I think it's more than that, though. Some kids just don't feel like they belong in any group yet. Even with the new games, they might still feel out of place."

Dano, who had been listening quietly, suddenly spoke up. "What if we focus on making the games about friendship? Like, what if the goal of the next game isn't about winning or completing a quest, but about helping each other out and working together to build something? Something that everyone can contribute to."

Ora's eyes lit up. "That's a great idea, Dano! If the goal is friendship and teamwork, it might make the kids who are on the sidelines feel more comfortable joining in. They won't feel like there's pressure to perform; they'll just be part of a bigger group."

"What kind of game could we do?" Remi asked, tapping her pencil against her notebook. "We've done adventure games and relay games. Maybe we could do something that involves more interaction between players—like building something together or solving something that requires *everyone* to pitch in."

Kiva suddenly smiled. "What if we make a game called **Bridge Builders**? The idea could be that all the kids have to work together to build 'bridges' that connect different parts of the playground. It could be a symbolic way of showing that we're trying to connect everyone."

Ora's face lit up with excitement. "I love it! We could make each bridge a different kind of task—like one could be a puzzle, another could be an obstacle course, and another could be something creative, like making up a team chant or song. The point would be to build connections between kids who haven't worked together before."

"And the best part is," Dano added, "everyone would need to work together to build each bridge. No one would be left out because there's always something for everyone to do."

The group continued brainstorming, adding details to the game. Each team would start at a different point on the playground, and their goal would be to "build" three bridges that connected their starting point to the other zones. To build each bridge, the team would have to complete a task—whether it was solving a puzzle, doing a physical challenge, or working together to create something fun. The catch was that they couldn't move on to the next bridge until *everyone* on the team had contributed to the current task.

By the time recess came the next day, Ora and her friends were ready to introduce *Bridge Builders* to the playground. They were nervous, but also excited, knowing this game could be the key to reaching the kids who still felt left out.

As soon as the bell rang, Ora and her friends gathered the kids near the big tree to explain the rules.

"Today, we're going to play a new game called *Bridge Builders*!" Ora announced. "The goal is to work together to build bridges that connect different parts of the playground. But instead of just racing to complete challenges, we're going to make sure that everyone has a role to play. You can't finish a bridge unless every team member helps out!"

The kids looked intrigued, and some of them began asking questions.

"So, it's like we're actually building something?" asked a girl named Lina, who had never joined in the games before.

"Sort of," Ora replied. "We're not physically building a real bridge, but we're building connections between each other by working as a team. For example, one bridge might involve solving a puzzle, and another might be a teamwork challenge where you have to help each other get across the 'river' by using balance and coordination. And don't worry, there are no winners or losers in this game—it's all about building together."

The idea of no winners or losers seemed to ease some of the kids' nerves, especially those who had been hesitant to join before. Sami and Althea, now confident leaders in their own right, were already excited to play and quickly volunteered to lead their teams.

As the kids divided into groups, Ora noticed that a few of the shyer kids, like Lina, were still hanging back. Determined not to leave anyone out, Ora approached Lina and some of the others.

"Hey, do you want to join our team?" Ora asked gently. "We could really use your help. I think you'd be great at solving one of the puzzles."

Lina looked surprised but smiled shyly. "I'll try."

With that, the game began. Each team headed to their starting zone, eager to start building their first "bridge." The first task involved solving a simple puzzle, which required the kids to figure out a riddle that led them to a hidden "plank" they needed to build their bridge.

Lina, who had been hesitant at first, quickly jumped in to help, offering ideas and working with her team to solve the riddle.

"I think the answer has something to do with the swings!" Lina exclaimed after thinking it through. "The riddle said something about 'flying without wings,' and that's the swings!"

Her team rushed over to the swings and found the hidden plank, cheering as they completed the first part of the bridge. Lina's face lit up with pride, and Ora smiled, knowing that this was exactly what they had hoped for—helping kids like Lina feel included and important.

Meanwhile, in another part of the playground, Kiva's team was working on the second bridge challenge—a physical task where they had to work together to balance on a series of stepping stones without falling off. Althea, who couldn't participate in the physical part of the challenge because of her wheelchair, took on the role of team leader, guiding her teammates and offering advice.

"Try moving your foot a little more to the left," Althea called out to her teammate. "You're almost there! And don't forget to help each other stay balanced!"

With Althea's leadership and encouragement, her team successfully completed the challenge, building their second bridge.

7 Lessons Learned from Chapter 10:

1. **Building connections is more important than winning**: *Bridge Builders* showed that games don't need to focus on competition; they can be about working together and making new friends.

2. **Everyone has something valuable to contribute**: Whether it's solving a puzzle, offering support, or leading a team, every child's role is important.

3. **Inclusivity fosters confidence**: When shy or hesitant kids are encouraged to join in, they gain confidence and feel valued as part of the group.

4. **Collaboration strengthens friendships**: By working together to build bridges, the kids learned how to support and rely on each other, creating stronger bonds.

5. **Leadership comes in many forms**: Althea couldn't physically complete the challenge, but she led her team with encouragement and guidance, proving that leadership isn't just about physical ability.

6. **Helping others creates a sense of belonging**: When kids work together to help their teammates succeed, they feel more connected and included.

7. **Inclusivity takes time and effort**: Creating a playground where everyone feels welcome requires constant attention and creativity, but it's worth it in the end.

Chapter 11: The Role of Teachers

As the games on the playground grew more popular and more inclusive, Ora and her friends were thrilled to see how much things had changed. Every day, more and more kids were joining in, and those who had once felt left out were becoming leaders and active participants in the new playground dynamic. However, Ora couldn't help but notice that despite their efforts, there were still areas where they could use more help. They had created new games, built bridges of friendship, and even tackled the exclusivity of the Big Slide. But they had yet to figure out how to make some of the physical spaces on the playground more accessible for everyone—especially kids like Althea, who still faced challenges when it came to moving freely around certain parts of the playground.

One day, as Ora was walking to school with Kiva, she voiced her concerns. "We've done a lot, but there are still some parts of the playground that Althea and others can't use. I've noticed that she avoids certain areas because they're hard for her to navigate in her wheelchair."

Kiva nodded thoughtfully. "Yeah, I've noticed that too. And even though we've made the Big Slide more welcoming, there are still places that not everyone can get to easily. It's not fair that some kids can't participate fully just because the playground wasn't designed for everyone."

Ora sighed. "I wish there was something more we could do. We've done our best to create games that include everyone, but we can't change the equipment ourselves."

As they approached the school gates, Kiva suddenly brightened. "What if we ask the teachers for help? They're always talking about how important it is for everyone to be included, right? Maybe they could help us make some changes to the playground itself."

Ora thought about it. They had focused so much on what they could do as kids—designing games, inviting others to play, and making sure everyone had a role—that they hadn't considered how the teachers might be able to support their efforts.

"You're right," Ora said, her eyes lighting up. "The teachers could help us! Maybe they can talk to the principal about getting new equipment or making adjustments to the playground. We should tell them what we've been doing and how they can help make the playground more accessible for everyone."

During recess that day, Ora and her friends gathered to discuss the idea. They decided to speak with Ms. Lopez, one of the teachers who always encouraged them to think about fairness and inclusion in their daily activities. Ms. Lopez was kind, approachable, and known for listening to students' ideas, so she seemed like the perfect person to talk to.

After school, Ora, Kiva, Remi, and Dano approached Ms. Lopez in her classroom. She was sitting at her desk, grading papers, but she smiled warmly when she saw them.

"Hi, Ms. Lopez," Ora began, a little nervously. "We wanted to talk to you about something important."

Ms. Lopez set down her pen and gave them her full attention. "Of course, Ora. What's on your mind?"

Ora explained everything—the games they had been organizing, the progress they had made in including more kids, and the challenges they still faced when it came to the physical structure of the playground.

"We've been working hard to make sure everyone feels included," Ora said, "but we've noticed that there are still parts of the playground that aren't easy for kids like Althea to use. We've created games that include everyone, but we can't change things like the equipment or the ground. We were hoping that maybe you could help us talk to the principal about making the playground more accessible."

Ms. Lopez listened carefully, nodding as Ora spoke. When Ora finished, she smiled, clearly impressed by what they had accomplished.

"I'm so proud of all of you," Ms. Lopez said. "You've done something really special by making sure the playground is a place where everyone can belong. It's not always easy to take on such a big challenge, but you've shown incredible leadership and creativity."

Ora and her friends beamed at the praise, but Ms. Lopez wasn't done.

"You're absolutely right," she continued. "The physical playground itself does need to be more inclusive, and that's something the school can help with. I'll speak with the principal and the school board about making improvements to the equipment and the layout, so that all kids—regardless of their abilities—can participate fully."

Ora felt a wave of relief wash over her. It felt good to know that they weren't in this alone and that the adults in the school were willing to help.

"Thank you so much, Ms. Lopez," Kiva said. "We've been trying to figure out what else we can do, but we knew we needed help from the school."

Ms. Lopez smiled again. "You've already done so much by creating these wonderful games and making sure everyone feels included. Now it's our turn to support you. I'll also see if we can get some new equipment installed—things like ramps, swings that are easier for everyone to use, and maybe even more accessible paths around the playground."

Ora's heart soared. This was exactly what they needed—real changes that would make the playground a better place for everyone.

Over the next few days, Ms. Lopez followed through on her promise. She arranged a meeting with the principal, and Ora and her friends were invited to present their ideas. At first, Ora was nervous about speaking in front of the principal and the school board, but with her friends by her side, she felt ready.

They created a simple presentation, showing how the playground could be improved with more accessible equipment and better layouts. They even suggested adding new play structures that were designed for kids of all abilities, like sensory play areas and swings with extra support. They explained how their games had already made a difference in bringing kids together, but they emphasized how much more they could do if the physical space was also designed to be inclusive.

The principal, Mr. Wilkins, listened intently as Ora and her friends spoke. He was clearly impressed by their dedication and creativity.

"I have to say," Mr. Wilkins said once they had finished, "I'm incredibly proud of what you've accomplished. You've done something that many adults struggle to do—create a community where everyone feels welcome. I think your ideas are fantastic, and I'm going to do everything I can to make sure the school supports your efforts. We'll work with the school board to start making some of these changes as soon as possible."

Ora and her friends could hardly believe it. They had hoped for some support, but the principal's enthusiastic response exceeded their expectations.

"Thank you so much, Mr. Wilkins," Ora said, her voice full of gratitude. "We just want to make sure the playground is a place where everyone feels like they belong."

Mr. Wilkins smiled warmly. "And that's exactly what you're doing. You're making this school a better place for everyone. I'm going to make sure we honor that by creating a playground that reflects those values."

7 Lessons Learned from Chapter 11:

1. **Asking for help is important**: Sometimes, big changes require support from others, including adults and teachers who can help make things happen.
2. **Teachers can be powerful allies**: Ms. Lopez and the

principal played a crucial role in helping Ora and her friends create a more inclusive playground.

3. **Inclusivity extends beyond games**: It's not just about the activities on the playground—physical spaces need to be designed with everyone in mind.

4. **Persistence leads to real change**: Ora and her friends didn't stop at creating inclusive games; they also worked to make lasting improvements to the playground itself.

5. **Leadership can come from kids**: The students took the lead in creating a more inclusive school environment, showing that kids can make a big impact.

6. **Community efforts bring about transformation**: The entire school, from teachers to students to the principal, worked together to create a more inclusive and welcoming playground.

7. **Small steps lead to big improvements**: By starting with games and friendship, Ora and her friends paved the way for larger, more permanent changes in the playground and the school as a whole.

Chapter 12: A Setback

Everything seemed to be going well for Ora and her friends. With the help of the teachers, changes were underway to make the playground more accessible, and their games were continuing to bring more kids together. The atmosphere on the playground was shifting, and Ora could feel the joy of seeing kids from all different backgrounds and abilities playing together.

But then, unexpectedly, things took a turn.

It happened during recess one sunny afternoon, while Ora, Sami, and Althea were leading another round of *Bridge Builders*. As usual, the kids were spread out across the different zones, working together to solve puzzles and complete challenges to "build" their bridges. Everything was going smoothly—until a disagreement broke out between two teams near the jungle gym.

Ora was nearby when she first heard the raised voices. She turned toward the sound and saw that Finn and Vex were on one team, while a boy named Caleb and his friends were on another. Both teams had been working on the same bridge challenge, but it looked like something had gone wrong.

"That's not fair!" Caleb shouted, his face flushed with frustration. "We were here first, and you guys are just pushing ahead without even following the rules!"

Finn crossed his arms, clearly annoyed. "We didn't break any rules. You're just mad because we finished the challenge before you did."

"That's because you cheated!" Caleb's teammate, a girl named Mia, added. "You weren't supposed to skip the puzzle and go straight to the next part. That's not how the game works!"

Vex, who had been standing off to the side, shrugged nonchalantly. "It's not our fault you're too slow. We figured out a faster way to do it."

Ora quickly walked over, trying to calm things down before it escalated any further. "Hey, what's going on?" she asked, stepping between the two groups.

"They're cheating!" Caleb said angrily, pointing at Finn and Vex. "They skipped the puzzle part of the bridge challenge and went straight to the physical task. We've been working on the puzzle for the last ten minutes, and they just went around us!"

"We didn't cheat," Finn shot back defensively. "We just didn't want to waste time on something that wasn't important. We're trying to win the game."

Ora frowned. She understood Caleb's frustration. The whole point of *Bridge Builders* was that every part of the challenge mattered, and each task was designed to involve different skills—puzzles, physical challenges, and creativity. By skipping the puzzle, Finn's team had undermined the spirit of the game, even if they hadn't technically broken any rules.

"Finn," Ora said calmly, "the point of the game isn't just to finish quickly. It's about working together and making sure everyone on your team has a role. Skipping parts of the challenge isn't fair to the other teams."

Finn rolled his eyes. "This is just a game, Ora. Why does it matter how we do it?"

Before Ora could respond, Vex chimed in. "Yeah, why are we making such a big deal out of it? We were just playing. If Caleb's team can't keep up, that's not our problem."

Ora opened her mouth to argue, but before she could say anything, Caleb's frustration boiled over. "You guys are the reason the playground was so messed up in the first place!" he yelled. "You always think you can do whatever you want, and no one else matters. This isn't your playground anymore!"

The accusation hung in the air, and for a moment, no one spoke. Finn looked taken aback, and Vex's smirk faded. Ora's heart sank as she realized that, despite all the progress they had made, there was still lingering resentment between some of the kids. It wasn't just about the game anymore—old wounds from when the playground was divided were resurfacing.

"I'm done," Caleb muttered, shaking his head in frustration. He and his team turned and walked away, leaving the bridge challenge unfinished.

Ora watched them go, feeling a knot of anxiety form in her stomach. She turned back to Finn and Vex, who looked equally uncomfortable.

"You're ruining everything," Mia said, her voice quieter now but still full of hurt. "We were finally starting to play together, and now it's going back to the way it was."

Finn said nothing, but Vex gave Ora a long look before turning away, clearly not in the mood to argue anymore. Both boys walked off, leaving Ora standing there with the sinking feeling that everything they had worked for was starting to fall apart.

As the recess bell rang and the kids returned to class, Ora felt defeated. She had thought that by creating new games and making the playground more inclusive, they had solved the problem of division and competition. But the argument between Finn and Caleb showed that the issues ran deeper than just who could play what game. There were still feelings of unfairness, jealousy, and mistrust lurking beneath the surface.

That afternoon, Ora and her friends gathered under the big tree after school to talk about what had happened.

"What are we going to do?" Remi asked, clearly worried. "It feels like all the progress we made just disappeared in one argument."

"I don't get why Finn and Vex are acting like this," Dano said, frowning. "They were finally starting to play along with everyone, and now it's like they're going back to their old ways."

Kiva sighed. "It's not just them, though. Caleb was right—there's still tension between some of the kids who used to be left out and the ones who were always in control. Even if Finn didn't technically cheat, skipping the puzzle felt unfair, like he was still trying to be better than everyone else."

Ora nodded. "I think there's more going on than just the game. Even though we've been working hard to include everyone, there are still kids who feel like the playground belongs to one group or another. There's still a lot of hurt from before."

"But we've done everything we could to make it fair!" Remi said, throwing her hands up. "What else can we do?"

For a moment, no one spoke. The weight of the situation hung heavily in the air. Ora knew that they had made incredible progress in making the playground more inclusive, but it was clear that there were deeper feelings of division that couldn't be fixed with just games. They needed to address those feelings head-on if they wanted the playground to truly be a place where everyone felt like they belonged.

Finally, Ora spoke up. "I think we need to have a real conversation about this—not just with Finn and his friends, but with everyone. We've been focusing on making sure everyone can play the games, but we haven't really talked about how people *feel* about the changes. I think some of the kids who used to have more control over the playground are feeling like they're losing something, and the kids who were left out still feel like things aren't fair."

Kiva nodded slowly. "That makes sense. We've been so focused on making sure everyone can play, we forgot to ask how they feel about the new rules and games. Maybe some kids feel like they're not being heard."

Remi looked thoughtful. "What if we organize a meeting with all the kids? A place where everyone can talk about how they feel about the changes. It doesn't have to be about the games, just a chance for everyone to share what's on their mind."

Dano smiled slightly. "Like a playground council?"

Ora's eyes lit up. "Exactly! We can invite kids from every group—Finn's friends, Caleb's team, Althea, Sami, and anyone else who wants to come. We'll give everyone a chance to talk about what they think is working and what isn't."

7 Lessons Learned from Chapter 12:

1. **Setbacks are a part of progress**: Even when things seem to be going well, challenges and conflicts can arise. Setbacks don't mean failure—they're opportunities to learn and grow.
2. **Unspoken feelings can cause tension**: Just because kids are playing together doesn't mean old feelings of division and unfairness have disappeared. These feelings need to be addressed directly.
3. **Fairness isn't just about rules**: Even if no one breaks the rules, actions that feel unfair to others can create resentment. Fairness means considering everyone's feelings and perspectives.
4. **Inclusivity goes beyond participation**: Creating an inclusive space isn't just about making sure everyone can play—it's also about making sure everyone feels heard and valued.
5. **Communication is key**: When conflicts arise, it's important to create a space where everyone can express their feelings and ideas without fear of judgment or blame.
6. **Leadership means listening**: Ora and her friends realized that being leaders on the playground wasn't just about organizing games—it was about making sure everyone's voice was heard.
7. **Perseverance is essential**: Even when things go wrong, it's important to keep working toward the goal of inclusivity and fairness. Setbacks are just part of the journey.

Chapter 13: The Power of Listening

The next morning, Ora felt a strange mixture of nerves and hope as she arrived at school. Today was the day of the playground council meeting—a chance for everyone to talk about the feelings and frustrations that had been bubbling beneath the surface for so long. Ora knew this meeting was crucial. If they didn't address the tension and division that still existed among the kids, all the progress they had made in creating an inclusive playground could unravel.

Ora and her friends had spent the previous afternoon preparing for the meeting. They had made posters inviting everyone to join them near the big tree at lunch, and they had explained the purpose of the meeting to the kids during recess. The goal wasn't to point fingers or place blame, but to listen—to give everyone a voice and figure out how they could make the playground a place where everyone truly felt they belonged.

By lunchtime, a small but diverse group of kids had gathered near the big tree. Ora was relieved to see that not only had kids like Althea, Sami, and Lina shown up, but so had Finn, Vex, and even Caleb, who had stormed off during the argument the previous day. Ora knew this was a good sign—if everyone was willing to talk, there was a chance they could find a solution together.

Ora stepped forward, taking a deep breath. "Thanks for coming, everyone," she began, her voice clear but a little shaky. "We've been working really hard to make the playground a place where everyone can play and feel included. But yesterday, we saw that there are still some problems. We realized that we haven't done enough to listen to how everyone is feeling about the changes. That's why we're here today. We want to hear what you think—what's been working, what hasn't, and how we can make things better for everyone."

Ora paused, glancing around at the circle of kids. There was a brief silence, and for a moment, she worried that no one would speak up.

But then Sami, who had grown much more confident over the past few weeks, raised his hand.

"I really like the new games we've been playing," Sami said quietly but confidently. "Before, I used to just stand on the side and watch, but now I feel like I belong. I like that we all have different roles, and it's not just about who's the fastest or the strongest."

Althea nodded in agreement. "Yeah, me too. I used to feel like I couldn't participate in a lot of the games because of my wheelchair, but now there are more ways for me to join in. I love solving puzzles and leading my team, and it makes me feel like I'm part of something."

Ora smiled, feeling encouraged by their words. But she knew this was only one side of the story.

"What about the rest of you?" she asked, turning toward Finn, Vex, and Caleb. "How do you feel about the changes?"

For a moment, Finn looked like he wasn't going to say anything. He glanced at Vex, who gave him a small nod, and then back at Ora. Finally, he spoke.

"I guess...I mean, the games are fine," Finn began, sounding unsure of himself. "But sometimes it feels like things aren't as fun as they used to be. Before, we could just play soccer or race down the Big Slide without thinking about all these new rules. Now it feels like everything has to be a team game, and sometimes I just want to do my own thing."

Ora listened carefully, nodding. "I understand that," she said. "You're saying you miss some of the games where you could be competitive or just play without having to think about working with a team, right?"

Finn nodded, looking a little relieved that Ora hadn't dismissed his feelings. "Yeah, exactly. I'm not trying to say that the new games are bad, but it feels like there's less room for just playing for fun, you know?"

Vex chimed in. "And it's not just that. Sometimes it feels like we're being told how to play, like we don't have a choice. I get that you want everyone to be included, but it feels like we've lost some of the freedom we had before."

Ora took a deep breath, thinking about what they were saying. She had been so focused on making the playground more inclusive that she hadn't considered how some kids might feel like they were being forced into a different way of playing—one that didn't leave room for the kinds of games they used to love.

"That makes sense," Ora said. "We wanted to create games that included everyone, but maybe we haven't left enough space for kids to play the way they used to—just for fun, without it always being about teamwork or roles. I think we can find a way to balance both."

Caleb, who had been quiet up until now, suddenly spoke up. "It's not just about that, though," he said, his voice tight with frustration. "I get that Finn and Vex want to play the way they used to, but some of us still feel like they're always in charge. Like, even when we're playing these new games, they're still the ones leading everything. It feels like nothing's really changed."

Finn looked taken aback. "That's not true! We've been playing the games just like everyone else!"

"Maybe," Caleb said, "but you still act like the games are all about you. Like yesterday, when you skipped the puzzle in *Bridge Builders*. You didn't even care about doing it the right way—you just wanted to win, like always."

Ora could see the tension rising between Finn and Caleb again, and she knew she had to step in before things got worse.

"Okay, let's take a step back," she said gently. "I think what Caleb is saying is that some kids still feel like they don't have as much control over the games, even though we've made changes. And I think Finn is saying that he misses having more freedom to play the way he's used to. Both of these things are valid."

Finn crossed his arms, looking frustrated. "But what are we supposed to do? Just let everyone else decide how we play?"

"No," Ora said. "I think we need to find a way to balance things out. We don't want anyone to feel like they don't belong or like they're not in control. Maybe we can come up with games that have a mix—some parts where we work as a team and other parts where everyone can do their own thing."

Vex, who had been listening quietly, nodded. "That could work. I mean, I like the team games, but I also miss just playing without having to think about it so much. Maybe we could switch things up sometimes—like have days where we play more competitive games and other days where it's about teamwork."

Ora smiled. "That's a great idea. We can have different types of games on different days, so there's something for everyone. And we can make sure that everyone gets a chance to lead or suggest ideas for the games, so it's not always the same people in charge."

Caleb, who still looked a little tense, sighed. "I just don't want things to go back to the way they were before. I like the changes, but it feels like it's still the same kids calling the shots."

"I get that," Ora said softly. "And we're going to keep working on making sure everyone feels like they have a voice. Maybe we can rotate who leads the games or who picks the challenges, so it's not always the same people in charge."

The kids around the circle began nodding in agreement, and for the first time in a while, Ora felt like they were making real progress—not just in terms of the games, but in how they communicated with each other.

As the meeting continued, more kids began sharing their thoughts. Some, like Sami and Althea, talked about how much they loved the new games and how included they felt. Others, like Finn and Caleb, shared their concerns about making sure there was room for both teamwork and individual play. And even the quieter kids, like Lina, spoke up about how they appreciated being given roles where they could contribute without feeling overwhelmed.

7 Lessons Learned from Chapter 13:

1. **Listening is a powerful tool**: By creating a space where everyone could share their feelings, Ora and her friends were able to address the underlying issues on the playground.
2. **Different perspectives matter**: It's important to consider how changes affect everyone, not just the majority.
3. **Inclusivity means balancing different needs**: Some kids enjoy competitive games, while others prefer teamwork. Both types of play can be included to make sure everyone is happy.
4. **Fairness isn't just about the rules**: Sometimes, even when things seem fair on the surface, feelings of unfairness can linger if certain kids feel like they don't have a voice.
5. **Communication prevents conflict**: Instead of letting frustrations build up, it's better to talk about problems openly so they can be addressed before they escalate.
6. **Leadership can be shared**: Rotating who leads the games or makes decisions helps ensure that everyone feels included and valued.
7. **Setbacks can lead to growth**: Facing challenges or disagreements doesn't mean the end of progress. In fact, it can be an opportunity to make things even better.

Chapter 14: Building a New Game Together

The day after the playground council meeting, Ora felt a sense of relief. The meeting had gone better than she had expected, and she was proud that they had created a space for everyone to share their feelings and ideas. But she also knew that the real work wasn't over. The next step was putting those ideas into action. They had listened, but now they needed to build something together that reflected what everyone wanted—a game that combined teamwork, individual play, and, most importantly, fun for all.

As she sat with her friends by the big tree during recess, they began brainstorming what this new game could be. The challenge was figuring out how to balance competition with inclusivity, and how to create a game where every kid—no matter their ability or personality—could feel like they were part of the action.

"We've done a lot of team-based games," Dano said, scratching his head thoughtfully. "But some kids still want more chances to show what they can do on their own."

"Yeah," Remi added, "but we also don't want to go back to the way things were before, where only the fastest or strongest kids had fun and everyone else felt left out."

Kiva, who had been sketching ideas in her notebook, suddenly looked up with a bright idea. "What if we design a game that has both individual challenges and team challenges? Like, each kid could have their own mini-challenge to complete, but the whole team still has to work together to finish the game."

Ora's eyes lit up. "That's a great idea! We could make it so that each player gets to do something they're good at, but the team can't win unless everyone completes their part. That way, no one is left out, and everyone's skills are important."

Remi grinned. "And we can have different kinds of mini-challenges—some physical, some mental, and some creative. That way, it's not just about who can run the fastest or jump the highest. Everyone will have a chance to shine."

The more they talked, the more the idea took shape. They decided to call the game **Skill Quest,** and it would involve a series of challenges that each player on a team had to complete. The twist was that each challenge was designed to highlight different skills—whether it was solving a puzzle, creating a short song or chant, completing an obstacle course, or working together to solve a riddle. Some tasks would require quick thinking, others would need teamwork, and a few would test physical skills—but every player would be able to choose a challenge that suited them best.

The game would also include a rule that each team couldn't move to the next challenge until every member had completed their individual task. This way, no one could be left behind, and every kid had a role in helping their team succeed.

After outlining the basic structure of *Skill Quest,* Ora and her friends felt a surge of excitement. They knew this game could be the perfect balance of competition and teamwork, and they couldn't wait to share it with the other kids.

During lunch, they spread the word about the new game, inviting everyone to join them for the first round of *Skill Quest* after recess. As the bell rang, signaling the start of recess, Ora was happy to see a large group of kids gathering near the big tree, curious and excited to play.

"Okay, everyone!" Ora called out, gathering the kids in a circle. "Today we're trying something new. It's called *Skill Quest,* and the goal is to complete a series of challenges—some by yourself, and some with your team. But here's the twist: you can't move on to the next challenge until every member of your team finishes their task. So it's not just about speed or strength—it's about making sure everyone gets a chance to help the team."

Ora explained the different types of challenges: there would be a puzzle-solving station for those who liked using their brains, an obstacle course for the more physical players, a creative challenge for the artistic kids, and a teamwork challenge where everyone would have to work together to solve a group problem. Each player would get to choose their own challenge, but they'd also have to support their teammates as they moved through the game.

The kids were buzzing with excitement as they divided into teams. Ora noticed that, for the first time, there wasn't any hesitation or tension between the different groups. Even Finn and his friends seemed eager to try the new game, and kids like Sami and Althea, who had thrived in the previous games, looked ready to take on their roles.

The first challenge was the obstacle course, which included a series of low hurdles, a balance beam, and a set of hoops to jump through. Finn and Vex were the first to tackle the course, showing off their physical skills as they raced through it with ease. But instead of gloating or racing ahead, they waited at the end of the course, cheering on the other kids who were still making their way through. Ora smiled as she watched them—Finn and Vex were starting to see the value in supporting their teammates, not just winning.

Meanwhile, Sami and Althea were working on the puzzle challenge. Althea, who loved solving riddles, quickly figured out the answer to the puzzle, while Sami helped guide the other kids who were struggling. Once they completed the puzzle, they moved to the creative challenge, where each team had to come up with a chant or song to motivate their group. Lina, who had been shy about participating in previous games, lit up during this challenge, leading her team in a simple but catchy chant that had everyone clapping and laughing along.

As the game progressed, Ora saw something incredible happening. Kids who had once been unsure of themselves—like Lina, Sami, and even some of the quieter kids from Caleb's group—were stepping up and taking on leadership roles in their teams. And the more confident kids, like Finn and Vex, were learning how to support their teammates instead of just focusing on their own success. Every team was working together, balancing individual effort with teamwork, and it was clear that *Skill Quest* was creating an atmosphere of mutual respect and cooperation.

By the time the game ended, the playground was filled with the sounds of laughter and cheering. Each team had completed their quest, and every player had contributed to the team's success. There were no arguments, no feelings of exclusion—just a sense of accomplishment and pride in what they had achieved together.

After recess, as the kids headed back to class, Finn approached Ora with a smile. "That was a pretty cool game," he said. "I liked that everyone got to do their own thing but still had to work together."

Ora grinned. "I'm glad you liked it. We wanted to make sure everyone had a chance to show what they could do, while still making it a team effort."

"Yeah," Finn nodded thoughtfully. "I didn't realize how much fun it could be to help the other kids out. I think Vex and I were too focused on winning before."

Ora appreciated his honesty. "I think we all learned a lot over the past few weeks. It's not just about winning—it's about making sure everyone feels like they're part of the game."

As Finn walked away to join his friends, Ora felt a deep sense of satisfaction. *Skill Quest* had been a success, and it had brought together kids from all different groups, allowing them to showcase their unique skills while still working as a team. The tension and competition that had once divided the playground seemed to be fading, replaced by a spirit of cooperation and friendship.

7 Lessons Learned from Chapter 14:

1. **Balancing individual and team play is important**: *Skill Quest* showed that kids can enjoy individual challenges while

still working as a team, creating a more inclusive and balanced game.

2. **Everyone has unique strengths**: By allowing each player to choose their own challenge, the game highlighted different skills, making sure that every kid had a chance to shine.

3. **Supporting teammates can be just as rewarding as winning**: Finn and Vex learned that helping their teammates succeed was just as satisfying as completing the challenges themselves.

4. **Inclusivity fosters leadership**: Kids who had been hesitant to lead before, like Sami and Lina, stepped up and took charge in their own ways, proving that everyone can be a leader.

5. **Creativity enhances teamwork**: The creative challenges, like writing chants and songs, brought out the best in the kids' imaginations and helped bond the teams together.

6. **Games can teach important life skills**: *Skill Quest* taught the kids valuable lessons about collaboration, communication, and how to balance individual effort with teamwork.

7. **Change takes time but is worth it**: Creating an inclusive playground wasn't easy, but the effort Ora and her friends put into listening to others and making adjustments paid off in the end.

Chapter 15: A Playground for Everyone

The success of *Skill Quest* marked a turning point on the playground. For the first time, Ora and her friends could see a real transformation taking place. The once divided playground, with its small cliques and exclusive zones, had become a place where kids of all abilities and backgrounds were playing together, helping one another, and having fun. Ora felt a deep sense of pride in what they had accomplished, but she also knew that their work wasn't finished.

As the days went on, Ora noticed that more kids were joining in the games, and the atmosphere on the playground was becoming lighter and more welcoming. But there was one group of kids Ora still worried about—those who didn't fit easily into the new dynamic, the ones who still sat on the sidelines, watching but not playing. Ora couldn't shake the feeling that they had missed something important. If the playground was truly going to be a place for *everyone,* these kids needed to feel included, too.

One afternoon, after school, Ora gathered her friends to talk about what they could do next.

"We've made a lot of progress," Ora said as they sat in her backyard, surrounded by sketchbooks and notes about their past games. "But I've been noticing something lately. There are still a few kids who haven't really joined in. They sit on the benches or at the edges of the playground, and even though they watch, they never play. I think we need to find a way to bring them in, too."

Kiva nodded thoughtfully. "Yeah, I've seen them, too. Some of them look like they want to join but are too shy, or maybe they're afraid they won't be good at the games."

"I think some kids just don't feel comfortable in big groups," Dano added. "Not everyone likes being in the middle of things, and that's okay. But we still need to make sure they feel like they can be part of the playground in their own way."

Remi tapped her pencil against her notebook. "Maybe we need to create spaces that aren't just about games. Like, what if we had areas where kids could be more creative, or places where they could just hang out and talk without feeling pressured to play?"

Ora's eyes lit up. "I love that idea! We've been focusing a lot on games, but not everyone likes to play in the same way. If we create spaces where kids can feel comfortable just being themselves—whether that's drawing, talking, or doing something else—they might feel more included."

The group began brainstorming ideas for these new spaces. They wanted to create places where kids could express themselves in different ways, whether through art, music, storytelling, or simply relaxing with friends. These spaces would give kids who weren't as into physical games a chance to feel like they belonged on the playground, too.

After much discussion, they came up with three new areas to add to the playground:

1. **The Creative Corner**: This would be a quiet area near the big tree, where kids could sit and draw, paint, or work on crafts together. They would provide simple art supplies, like colored pencils, markers, and paper, and encourage kids to create whatever they wanted. There would also be a big mural wall where kids could add their drawings over time, creating a community art project.

2. **The Story Circle**: Located in a cozy nook near the garden, this space would be for kids who loved to tell stories or listen to others. They could take turns making up stories or reading aloud from books, and it would be a calm, relaxed place where kids could connect through their imaginations. Althea was especially excited about this space, as she loved reading and had always wanted to share her stories with others.

3. **The Friendship Bench**: This was an idea Kiva had come up

with after seeing some kids sit alone at recess. The Friendship Bench would be a special bench in the center of the playground, painted in bright, inviting colors. The idea was that if any kid felt lonely or wanted to make a new friend, they could sit on the bench, and other kids would know to come over and talk to them or invite them to play.

The next day, they brought their ideas to Ms. Lopez, who had been their biggest supporter throughout their playground transformation. As expected, she was thrilled with their new plans.

"These are wonderful ideas," Ms. Lopez said with a smile. "I love how you're thinking about all the different ways kids might want to participate. Not everyone likes to play physical games, and creating spaces where they can express themselves creatively or just relax with friends is a great way to include everyone."

Ms. Lopez promised to help them get the materials they needed to create the new spaces, and she even suggested involving the other teachers to spread the word to all the students. Ora and her friends were excited to see their vision coming to life. They spent the next few days preparing the new spaces, gathering art supplies, and painting the Friendship Bench with bright colors and positive words like "Welcome," "Friendship," and "Kindness."

When everything was ready, they unveiled the new areas during recess. The reaction was immediate and positive. Kids flocked to the Creative Corner, excited to draw and add their art to the mural wall. Althea led the way to the Story Circle, where she read aloud from one of her favorite books while other kids sat around, listening quietly. And the Friendship Bench—bright and cheerful in the middle of the playground—became a gathering spot for kids looking for a friend to talk to or someone to play with.

Ora watched with pride as the playground transformed yet again. It wasn't just about games anymore—it was about creating spaces where every kid, no matter their interests, could find a place to belong. The kids who had once sat on the sidelines, too shy or unsure to join in the games, were now finding their own ways to participate, whether through art, storytelling, or simply sitting on the bench and making new friends.

That afternoon, as Ora walked around the playground checking on the new spaces, she noticed a boy named Mateo sitting quietly at the Friendship Bench. Mateo had always been one of the quieter kids at school, and Ora realized she had never seen him join in any of the games. He was always on the sidelines, watching but never participating.

Ora approached him with a smile. "Hey, Mateo. How's it going?"

Mateo looked up, a little surprised to be noticed. "I'm okay," he said softly. "I just...didn't really have anyone to play with today."

Ora sat down next to him on the bench. "That's what this bench is for," she said gently. "If you're ever feeling left out, you can sit here, and someone will come over to talk to you or invite you to play. You don't have to be alone."

Mateo looked around at the other kids, who were playing and laughing together, and then back at Ora. "I guess I've never really known how to join in. I'm not very good at sports or games."

"That's okay," Ora said. "You don't have to be good at sports or games to have fun. There are lots of other things to do, like drawing in the Creative Corner or listening to stories in the Story Circle. And if you ever want to try a game, we'll make sure it's something you feel comfortable with. You belong here, Mateo."

Mateo smiled, a little more confident now. "Maybe I'll check out the Story Circle later," he said. "I like listening to stories."

"That sounds great," Ora said, standing up and offering him a hand. "And if you ever want to join a game, just let me know. We'd love to have you."

As Ora walked away, she felt a warmth in her heart. The playground was becoming a place where every kid, even the quiet ones like Mateo, could find their place. It wasn't just about the games or the activities—it was about building a community where everyone felt welcome, valued, and included.

7 Lessons Learned from Chapter 15:

1. **Inclusivity means more than just games**: Creating spaces for creativity, storytelling, and friendship allows kids with different interests to feel included, not just those who enjoy physical games.

2. **Quiet kids need spaces too**: By creating areas like the Story Circle and the Friendship Bench, Ora and her friends made sure that even shy or quiet kids had a place where they could connect with others.

3. **Creativity fosters community**: The Creative Corner and the community mural project gave kids a chance to express themselves and contribute to something bigger, fostering a sense of belonging.

4. **Friendship can be encouraged**: The Friendship Bench became a way for kids who felt alone to connect with others, helping to prevent feelings of isolation.

5. **Everyone has a role to play**: Whether through games, art, stories, or conversation, every child can contribute to the playground community in their own way.

6. **Belonging takes many forms**: The new playground spaces showed that belonging doesn't always mean playing games—sometimes it means simply being part of a shared space.

7. **Ongoing effort is needed for inclusion**: Ora and her friends understood that creating an inclusive playground is an ongoing process, and they were committed to continuing

their efforts to make the playground better for everyone.

Chapter 16: A Surprise Visitor

A few weeks had passed since the introduction of the Creative Corner, Story Circle, and Friendship Bench, and the playground was thriving in ways Ora and her friends could have only dreamed of. There was a sense of unity on the playground that had never existed before. Even though kids still played in their favorite zones and games, there was no more division or exclusion. Whether you wanted to run in a race, solve a puzzle, paint a picture, or tell a story, there was always a place for you.

One sunny afternoon, as Ora sat by the big tree watching kids play, she noticed Ms. Lopez approaching with someone unfamiliar by her side. The woman looked friendly and curious, with a notepad in hand and a camera slung around her neck. Ora's curiosity was piqued. Ms. Lopez hadn't mentioned any visitors today, and this woman definitely wasn't one of the usual teachers or staff.

"Hey, Ora," Ms. Lopez said with a warm smile as she approached. "I'd like you to meet someone. This is Ms. Hartman. She's a journalist writing a story about how schools are making playgrounds more inclusive."

Ora's eyes widened in surprise. A journalist? Writing a story about *their* playground?

Ms. Hartman smiled brightly and knelt down to Ora's level. "I've been hearing some wonderful things about the changes you and your friends have made to this playground," she said. "I came to see it for myself and hear the story from the people who made it happen."

Ora blushed, not used to the attention. "Oh, it wasn't just me," she said modestly. "It was a team effort. We all worked together to make sure the playground was a place where everyone could play."

Ms. Lopez gestured toward the playground, where kids were scattered across different zones—some climbing the jungle gym, others drawing at the Creative Corner, while a few sat in the Story Circle listening to Althea read. "I think Ms. Hartman would love to hear how it all started," Ms. Lopez said. "How you and your friends came up with the idea and what changes you've made."

Ora felt a mix of excitement and nervousness as she explained the journey. She told Ms. Hartman how it all began with noticing that not everyone felt welcome on the playground—how some kids, like Sami and Althea, had been left out of games, and how certain areas, like the Big Slide, had become exclusive zones dominated by a few kids. She explained how they had started small, designing games like *Treasure Island* and *Adventure Quest* to include everyone, regardless of their abilities or interests.

"We just wanted to make sure that no one felt left out," Ora said, glancing over at the Friendship Bench, where a few kids were sitting together, chatting happily. "We realized that it wasn't just about the games—it was about creating spaces where everyone could feel comfortable, whether they wanted to run and play or just sit and talk."

Ms. Hartman listened intently, jotting down notes as Ora spoke. "It sounds like you've created more than just an inclusive playground—you've built a community," she said with admiration in her voice.

Ora smiled, feeling a sense of pride. "Yeah, I guess we have."

Just then, Sami, Kiva, and Dano approached, curious about the visitor. Ms. Lopez waved them over and introduced them to Ms. Hartman. After hearing about the article, Sami's eyes widened in surprise.

"You're writing about our playground?" Sami asked, a mix of excitement and disbelief in his voice.

Ms. Hartman nodded. "That's right! I think what you've done here is really special, and I want other schools to hear about it. Maybe your story will inspire other kids to make their playgrounds more inclusive too."

Kiva, always quick to offer ideas, spoke up. "We didn't just change the games—we made sure there were different kinds of spaces for everyone. Like the Creative Corner for kids who like to draw and the Story Circle for kids who love books and storytelling. We wanted to make sure there was something for everyone."

Dano chimed in, pointing toward the colorful Friendship Bench. "And that's the Friendship Bench. If someone feels lonely or doesn't know who to play with, they can sit there, and someone will come over and talk to them or invite them to play."

Ms. Hartman's eyes sparkled with interest. "That's a brilliant idea," she said, taking a photo of the bench. "It's such a simple concept, but it makes a big difference. I can see how you've really thought about how to include everyone."

As the kids talked, more students gathered around, intrigued by the visitor with the camera. Even Finn and Vex, who had once been resistant to the changes, joined the conversation. Ms. Hartman asked them what they thought about the new playground, and Finn, who had grown a lot since the early days of resisting change, spoke thoughtfully.

"At first, I didn't really get it," Finn admitted. "I thought things were fine the way they were, and I liked the games we used to play. But now, I see that we were leaving people out without even realizing it. The new games have been a lot more fun because we're all playing together, and I like that everyone has a chance to do something they're good at."

Vex nodded in agreement. "Yeah, and it's not just about who's the fastest or strongest anymore. We're all part of the team, and that's what makes it fun."

Ms. Hartman looked impressed. "It sounds like the changes have brought everyone closer together," she said. "What advice would you give to kids at other schools who want to make their playgrounds more inclusive?"

Ora thought for a moment, and then she smiled. "I'd tell them to start small. You don't have to change everything all at once. We started by just making new games that everyone could play. Once people saw how much fun it was to include everyone, the rest came naturally. And you have to listen to each other—like, really listen. It's not just about making rules; it's about understanding how everyone feels and what they need."

"And it helps to have adults who support you," Kiva added, nodding toward Ms. Lopez. "Ms. Lopez and the other teachers helped us talk to the principal, and now we're even getting new equipment to make the playground more accessible."

Ms. Hartman took down every word, her excitement clear. "I think your story is going to inspire a lot of people," she said. "I can't wait to write about it."

As she prepared to leave, Ms. Hartman asked for one final picture of the group. The kids gathered near the Friendship Bench, with Ora and her friends in the center, surrounded by the other students. Even Ms. Lopez joined in, standing proudly behind the kids who had transformed the playground into a place for everyone.

The photo captured more than just smiling faces—it captured the spirit of the playground, the unity and friendship that had grown from a simple idea of inclusion.

After Ms. Hartman left, the kids returned to their games, but Ora felt a sense of accomplishment that was deeper than before. The playground wasn't just a success for their school—it was something that could spread to other places, other kids who might be struggling with the same challenges they had faced.

7 Lessons Learned from Chapter 16:

1. **Small actions can have big impacts**: What started as a simple idea to make games more inclusive turned into something much bigger, creating a sense of community on the playground.
2. **Inclusivity benefits everyone**: Even kids who had resisted

the changes, like Finn and Vex, realized how much more fun it is when everyone can participate.

3. **Listening to others is key to building a strong community**: The success of the playground was rooted in the kids' ability to listen to each other's needs and ideas.

4. **Creative spaces can make a difference**: The addition of the Creative Corner, Story Circle, and Friendship Bench helped ensure that kids who weren't as interested in games could still find their place.

5. **Support from adults is crucial**: Ms. Lopez's support and involvement helped Ora and her friends take their ideas to the next level, showing how important it is for adults to encourage kids' initiatives.

6. **Sharing stories can inspire change**: By telling their story, Ora and her friends could inspire other schools to make their playgrounds more inclusive, proving that their efforts had an impact beyond just their own community.

7. **Inclusivity is an ongoing process**: The playground may have transformed, but Ora and her friends knew that there was always more work to be done to keep making it better for everyone.

Chapter 17: A New Challenge

With the playground now transformed into a welcoming space for everyone, life at Sunnyhill Elementary had become brighter and more harmonious. Every day, kids from all different backgrounds and abilities found something they enjoyed—whether it was creating art in the Creative Corner, telling stories in the Story Circle, or playing games like *Skill Quest* and *Treasure Island*. The playground had become a symbol of what was possible when inclusion, creativity, and teamwork came together.

But just when Ora thought things were settling into a happy routine, a new challenge appeared—one that Ora and her friends hadn't anticipated.

It started one afternoon when Ora overheard a conversation between two older kids near the Friendship Bench. They weren't regulars on the playground and didn't usually join the games, so their voices stood out.

"This playground is so...boring now," one of the older kids said, kicking the dirt by the bench. "Everything's about 'working together' and 'being fair.' What happened to just playing?"

His friend nodded in agreement. "Yeah, where's the fun in all these new rules? No more races, no more real competition. It's all too nice."

Ora, who had been standing nearby with Sami, felt a pang of frustration. She had thought the changes they'd made were for the better—making sure no one was left out, creating games that were fun for everyone, and building spaces where kids could connect. But here were these older kids, dismissing all of that as "boring."

Sami, noticing Ora's troubled expression, nudged her. "Don't let them get to you," he said quietly. "We know the playground's better now. Just because they don't like it doesn't mean it's bad."

But Ora couldn't shake the feeling that there might be something more to what the older kids were saying. They weren't the only ones who had grown bored with the playground's new structure. In recent weeks, a few other kids had mentioned that they missed the more competitive games, the races, and the excitement of winning. Even Finn and Vex, despite embracing the new changes, had quietly voiced similar concerns to Ora.

"What if they're right?" Ora whispered to Sami. "What if we've gone too far? We worked so hard to make sure everyone felt included, but maybe we forgot that some kids still like competition. We didn't think about how to keep things exciting for them."

Sami furrowed his brow. "I don't think we went too far, but maybe there's a way to bring back some of the excitement without going back to the old days, where only some kids got to have fun."

Ora nodded thoughtfully. "Maybe you're right. There has to be a way to balance the competition some kids want with the inclusivity we've worked so hard to build. We just need to find the right mix."

Later that day, Ora called a meeting with her usual group under the big tree to talk about the problem. She explained what she had overheard and shared her worries.

"I think we've done an amazing job," Ora began, "but I've been hearing from some of the older kids that they're feeling bored. They miss the thrill of competition—the excitement of races and winning. But I don't want to go back to the way things were, where only a few kids had fun and the rest were left out."

Kiva nodded in agreement. "I've heard that too. Some kids just don't enjoy the slower, more cooperative games as much. But I think we can find a way to make everyone happy without losing what we've built."

"I've been thinking," Dano said, speaking up. "What if we bring back some of the competitive elements but in a way that still keeps things fair? Like, maybe we could organize a playground tournament, but with different types of challenges—some physical, some creative, and some that require teamwork. That way, even if it's competitive, there's something for everyone."

Remi's eyes lit up. "That's a great idea! We could have different categories—races, puzzle challenges, creative tasks—and make sure each team has kids with different strengths. Everyone would still have to work together, but there would be a competitive edge to it."

Ora felt a surge of excitement. This could be the perfect solution—a way to reintroduce competition without leaving anyone out. The idea of a tournament that combined teamwork, creativity, and individual effort felt like the natural next step for their playground.

They spent the rest of the afternoon sketching out the idea. The tournament, which they decided to call **The Playground Games**, would be a mix of challenges that tested different skills: speed, strength, strategy, and creativity. Teams would compete in relay races, obstacle courses, puzzle-solving, and even a creative challenge where they had to come up with the best team chant or flag. The key difference from traditional competitions was that the teams would be mixed—each team would have kids with different abilities, and no one would be left out. Winning wouldn't just be about being the fastest or strongest; it would be about how well each team worked together, using everyone's strengths.

Once the plan was in place, Ora and her friends presented the idea to Ms. Lopez, who, as always, was thrilled to support them.

"I love it!" Ms. Lopez said with enthusiasm. "A tournament that celebrates both competition and teamwork? It's the perfect way to keep things fun while still maintaining the inclusive spirit you've worked so hard to build."

Ms. Lopez helped them organize the tournament and spread the word around the school. Soon, excitement started to build. Kids who had been missing the thrill of competition were eager to sign up, while those who loved the new collaborative games were excited to see how the tournament would work. The Playground Games would take place at the end of the week, and teams were already forming, buzzing with anticipation.

When the day of the tournament arrived, the energy on the playground was electric. Banners with team names fluttered in the breeze, and kids wore homemade armbands to show their team colors. Even the older kids, who had complained about the lack of competition, were getting into the spirit, eager to see how the new format would work.

Ora and her friends had created four main events for the tournament:

1. **The Great Relay**: A mix of running, jumping, and coordination. Each team member had to complete a section of the course, whether it was a sprint, a balance challenge, or navigating through a series of cones.
2. **The Puzzle Path**: Teams had to work together to solve a series of riddles and logic puzzles, with each correct answer unlocking the next part of the challenge.
3. **Creative Challenge**: Each team had to design a team flag and create a chant that represented their group. The challenge was judged on creativity, enthusiasm, and teamwork.
4. **The Final Race**: This was a physical challenge, but with a twist—each team had to carry a large inflatable ball across the field while making sure every teammate had a turn guiding the ball. Speed was important, but so was coordination and teamwork.

As the tournament began, the playground was filled with cheers, laughter, and a sense of friendly competition. The teams were diverse, with kids of all abilities working together to tackle each challenge. Ora watched with pride as kids who had once been unsure of themselves—like Sami, Althea, and Lina—took on leadership roles, guiding their teams through the puzzles and cheering them on during the races.

Even Finn and Vex, who had missed the more competitive games, were fully engaged in the tournament, but this time, they were using their skills to support their teams rather than just focusing on winning. Ora noticed that Finn had grown into a real leader, helping his teammates with the physical challenges and making sure everyone had a role to play.

The most exciting moment came during the Final Race. Two teams were neck and neck, with kids scrambling to guide the giant inflatable ball toward the finish line. Ora's team was slightly behind, but she noticed that their teamwork was stronger—every kid was cheering each other on, working together to keep the ball moving steadily. In the end, they didn't win the race, but they finished strong, with smiles on everyone's faces.

As the tournament came to a close, Ms. Lopez gathered everyone together near the big tree for the awards ceremony. But instead of handing out prizes for first, second, or third place, she and the teachers gave out special awards for teamwork, creativity, leadership, and perseverance. Every team was recognized for their unique strengths, and there were no losers—only kids who had worked together and had fun.

After the ceremony, Finn came over to Ora with a grin on his face. "You know, I didn't think I'd like these new games at first," he admitted. "But this tournament was awesome. It felt good to compete again, but in a different way."

7 Lessons Learned from Chapter 17:

1. **Balance is key**: The Playground Games showed that it's possible to balance competition and inclusivity, making sure everyone has fun without leaving anyone out.
2. **Listening to feedback is important**: Ora and her friends

took the feedback from the older kids and found a way to incorporate their desire for competition while still maintaining a focus on teamwork and inclusion.

3. **Leadership evolves**: Kids like Finn and Vex, who had once been focused only on winning, grew into leaders who supported their teammates and helped everyone succeed.

4. **Friendly competition can bring people together**: By designing the tournament to celebrate different strengths, the kids learned that competition doesn't have to divide—it can unite.

5. **Creativity can be part of competition**: The creative challenges in the tournament gave kids a chance to showcase their artistic and imaginative sides, proving that competition isn't just about physical abilities.

6. **Recognition matters**: The awards for teamwork, creativity, and leadership highlighted that success comes in many forms, not just winning.

7. **Inclusivity requires ongoing effort**: Ora and her friends realized that creating an inclusive playground is a process, and it's important to keep adapting to meet everyone's needs.

Chapter 18: The New Kid

The Playground Games had been a huge success, bringing new life to the playground and showing that competition and inclusivity could coexist. Ora and her friends felt more confident than ever that they had created a lasting community on the playground. But just when things seemed to be running smoothly, the arrival of a new student introduced a challenge they hadn't faced before.

His name was Rafi, and he arrived at Sunnyhill Elementary one crisp autumn morning. He was quiet, with a serious expression, and he didn't speak much during class. The teachers introduced him as having just moved to the area, but beyond that, little was said. Ora noticed him immediately. Something about the way he sat alone at recess, watching the other kids play, reminded her of how Sami and Althea had been before the changes to the playground. But there was something different about Rafi—he didn't just seem shy or unsure. He seemed guarded, like he didn't want anyone to approach him.

Ora's friends noticed too.

"Have you seen the new kid?" Kiva asked as they gathered by the big tree for recess that day. "He just sits by himself. I tried waving at him earlier, but he just looked away."

"I don't think he's interested in joining the games," Dano said. "Maybe he just needs more time to adjust. It's gotta be hard moving to a new school."

Sami nodded thoughtfully. "Yeah, it can be tough being the new kid. I remember when I first moved here—I didn't know how to make friends, and I felt like I didn't belong."

"But we don't want him to feel left out," Ora said, glancing over at Rafi, who was sitting on the edge of the playground, staring down at the ground. "We've worked so hard to make sure everyone feels welcome here. We can't let anyone slip through the cracks."

Remi looked over at Rafi and then back at Ora. "Maybe we should go talk to him. See if he wants to join us."

Ora hesitated. She had a feeling that Rafi wasn't the type to open up easily. He seemed distant, even withdrawn, and she didn't want to make him feel uncomfortable by overwhelming him. But she also knew that they couldn't just ignore him.

"Let's approach it slowly," Ora suggested. "We'll invite him to play, but we won't push too hard. Maybe if he sees that we're open to including him, he'll come around when he's ready."

The group agreed, and they decided to start with something simple. That afternoon, as the other kids spread out across the playground, Ora and her friends approached Rafi. He was sitting on a bench near the Friendship Bench but hadn't sat on it himself. His shoulders were hunched, and he seemed lost in thought.

"Hey, Rafi," Ora said gently, stopping a few feet away from him. "We're about to start a game of *Skill Quest*. Do you want to join us?"

Rafi looked up, his expression unreadable. For a moment, Ora thought he might get up and leave, but instead, he shook his head.

"No, thanks," he muttered, looking back down at his shoes.

Ora exchanged a glance with Kiva, who gave a small nod of understanding. They didn't want to push him, but they also didn't want to leave him completely alone.

"That's okay," Ora said kindly. "If you change your mind, we'll be over by the big tree. You're welcome to join anytime."

Without waiting for a response, Ora and her friends walked away, giving Rafi his space. They returned to their usual spot and started the game of *Skill Quest,* but Ora kept an eye on Rafi from a distance. He didn't move from the bench, but she could tell he was watching, even if he didn't want to admit it.

As the game continued, the kids ran through different challenges, cheering each other on as they completed their tasks. But Rafi stayed where he was, always watching but never joining in. Ora's heart ached a little as she thought about how hard it must be for him to be in a new school, feeling like an outsider.

The next day, Ora noticed something new. As she walked into the schoolyard before the bell, she spotted Rafi with his backpack slung over one shoulder, standing near the jungle gym. A few kids were climbing and playing, but Rafi wasn't interacting with them. Instead, he seemed to be observing them closely.

Ora thought for a moment, then approached him, determined to try again.

"Hey, Rafi," she said with a smile. "We're going to set up another game later. I was thinking, maybe you could help us decide what the next challenge should be. You've been watching a lot of the games, and you might have some good ideas."

Rafi looked startled, as if he hadn't expected anyone to speak to him. For a second, he didn't respond, and Ora was about to turn away, assuming he wasn't interested. But then, he surprised her.

"I don't know," he said quietly. "I'm not really good at these kinds of games."

Ora tilted her head. "You don't have to be good at them to have fun. We can find something that fits what you're comfortable with. We're always looking for new ideas."

Rafi seemed to consider this, but his face remained uncertain. "I just don't really...do games like that."

Ora sensed that pushing him further wouldn't help, so she backed off for now. "That's cool," she said, keeping her tone light. "If you ever feel like giving it a try, let me know. We could always use more players."

She smiled at him again and walked back to her friends, but she couldn't help but wonder what Rafi's story was. Why was he so hesitant to join in? Was it just because he was new, or was there something more?

Later that day, Ora met with her friends to discuss how things were going with Rafi.

"He still doesn't want to join," Ora said, sitting cross-legged on the grass near the big tree. "I feel like he's watching us, but he's not ready to participate."

Kiva frowned. "Maybe we should try something different. What if instead of asking him to join the games, we invite him to help out in another way? Like, he could help organize the games or design the next challenge. Maybe if he feels like he's contributing, he'll feel more comfortable."

"I like that idea," Dano said. "If he's shy about playing, maybe we can show him that there are other ways to be part of the group."

Remi nodded in agreement. "Yeah, and if he sees that we value his input, it might help him open up more."

The next day, Ora decided to put the plan into action. At recess, she approached Rafi again, this time with a different offer.

"Hey, Rafi," she said as she walked up to him near the swings. "We're thinking about creating a new game soon, but we need some fresh ideas. I was wondering if you'd like to help us come up with something. You've been watching a lot of what we do, and I bet you have some great ideas."

Rafi looked at her, his expression guarded. "You really want my ideas?" he asked, sounding surprised.

"Of course!" Ora said sincerely. "We're always trying to make the playground more fun for everyone, and we love getting input from different people. It doesn't have to be a game you play—you can help design it, and we'll test it out."

For the first time since arriving at the school, Rafi's expression softened. He seemed intrigued by the idea, even though he still looked hesitant. After a long pause, he finally nodded. "I guess I could try," he said quietly.

7 Lessons Learned from Chapter 18:

1. **Some kids need time and space to feel comfortable**: Rafi's

reluctance to join the games showed that not everyone is ready to participate right away, and it's important to be patient and understanding.

2. **There are many ways to be part of a community**: By inviting Rafi to help design the games instead of playing, Ora showed that there are different ways to contribute and feel included.

3. **Approaching slowly can build trust**: Rather than pushing Rafi to join right away, Ora and her friends took a more gentle approach, allowing him to open up on his own terms.

4. **Creativity can bridge gaps**: Rafi's creative ideas helped him connect with the group, showing that imagination and strategy can be just as valuable as physical skills.

5. **Everyone has something unique to offer**: Rafi's scavenger hunt idea brought a fresh perspective to the group, proving that every kid has their own strengths and ideas.

6. **Inclusivity is an ongoing effort**: Even after transforming the playground, Ora and her friends realized that there's always more work to do to ensure everyone feels welcome.

7. **Small steps lead to big changes**: Rafi's willingness to contribute to the group's plans was a small but significant step toward him feeling like part of the playground community.

Chapter 19: The Scavenger Hunt Adventure

The next day, excitement buzzed through the air as word spread that Ora and her friends were planning a scavenger hunt based on Rafi's ideas. It was a fresh, new challenge for the kids at Sunnyhill Elementary, something they hadn't done before, and the combination of physical tasks, puzzles, and hidden clues had everyone curious.

Rafi, who had been so quiet and reserved when he first arrived, now had a more visible presence on the playground. He still didn't join in the games as much, but he was slowly warming up to the group, especially now that they were using his ideas for the scavenger hunt. Ora could see the pride in his eyes, though he tried to hide it behind his usual quiet demeanor.

On the morning of the scavenger hunt, Ora and her friends gathered under the big tree to finalize the details. They had spent the last few afternoons preparing for the event, setting up clues and tasks all around the playground. Each clue would lead the teams to a different zone, where they would face a challenge that required a mix of physical, creative, and problem-solving skills.

"We'll have four teams," Ora explained to the group, pointing at the map of the playground they had drawn. "Each team will start in a different zone. The first team to find all the clues and solve the final puzzle wins, but remember—the point is to work together. No one can solve all the clues on their own."

Kiva nodded. "Each zone has a different kind of challenge. Some will be puzzles, others will be physical tasks like the obstacle course. And we've made sure every team has kids with different strengths, so everyone has a role to play."

Remi grinned. "I think this is going to be our best game yet. It's got a little bit of everything!"

Rafi stood nearby, watching the preparations with his arms crossed. He still hadn't fully joined in the games, but Ora could tell he was eager to see how his scavenger hunt idea would turn out.

When the bell rang for recess, the kids gathered around the big tree, excited and ready to begin. Teams were quickly divided, with Sami, Althea, Finn, and Lina each leading a group. Ora was especially happy to see Rafi quietly joining one of the teams. He wasn't the leader, but he was participating, and that was a big step for him.

Ms. Lopez had agreed to be the official "judge" for the scavenger hunt, making sure everyone followed the rules and giving the final approval when teams completed the challenges.

"All right, everyone," Ms. Lopez called out, clapping her hands to get the kids' attention. "This scavenger hunt is all about teamwork, creativity, and using your brains as much as your muscles. Each team will need to complete a series of challenges, and every member has to contribute to the final puzzle. Are you ready?"

The kids cheered in response, the excitement palpable.

With a nod from Ms. Lopez, the scavenger hunt began.

The first challenge for Ora's team was a puzzle set up near the Creative Corner. Hidden among the art supplies was a riddle that the team had to solve to move on to the next clue. Ora, Sami, and the other kids crowded around the riddle, trying to figure it out.

"What has keys but can't open a door?" Lina read aloud, frowning as she tried to think of the answer.

Sami's eyes lit up as he realized the answer. "It's a piano! Pianos have keys, but they don't open doors!"

"Nice one, Sami!" Ora said, giving him a high-five. With the answer in hand, they found the next clue hidden under the piano in the Creative Corner, and they were off to their next challenge.

Meanwhile, in the Forest Zone, Kiva's team was working on a physical challenge. They had to cross a series of "stepping stones" without touching the ground, using balance and coordination to make it to the other side. Finn, who was on Kiva's team, took the lead, hopping from one stone to the next with ease. But instead of rushing ahead, he stopped halfway to help the others.

"Take it slow," Finn said, offering his hand to a younger teammate who was struggling to keep their balance. "You've got this. Just focus one step at a time."

Kiva smiled as she watched Finn encouraging the others. It was moments like this that showed how much he had grown since the old days when he used to care only about winning.

Over by the jungle gym, Althea's team faced a creative challenge. They had to work together to create a chant that represented their team spirit, and Althea, who loved coming up with ideas, quickly took charge.

"Let's make it simple but catchy," Althea suggested, scribbling ideas in her notebook. "We could do something like 'We're the best, we can't be beat, our teamwork's strong, we'll take the heat!'"

The other kids clapped along as they practiced their chant, each one adding their own flair to the rhythm. Althea grinned, feeling proud of how well they were working together.

As the scavenger hunt continued, Ora's team made their way to the final zone, where the last clue awaited. They had solved puzzles, completed physical tasks, and even come up with a creative team chant. Now, they just needed to crack the final puzzle to win.

When they arrived at the last challenge, they found Rafi standing near the puzzle, watching as the teams approached. It was a simple puzzle—five pieces that, when put together, formed the map of the playground. But the catch was that each team member had to take turns placing the pieces in the correct order, relying on each other's observations and memory from the scavenger hunt.

Ora's team huddled together, each of them studying the puzzle pieces carefully. Sami pointed to one of the pieces. "That one's the

Creative Corner," he said confidently. "I remember the tree in the background."

Lina picked up another piece, nodding. "This one's the jungle gym—it's right next to the swings."

Slowly but surely, they worked together to fit the pieces in place. Just as they were finishing, Ora glanced up and saw Rafi watching them closely. She caught his eye and smiled, motioning for him to come over.

"Hey, Rafi, we could use your help with the last piece," she called out.

Rafi hesitated for a moment, then slowly walked over to the team. He looked at the puzzle, then at the final piece in his hand.

"I think this one goes here," he said quietly, placing the last piece in the center of the map, completing the puzzle.

The team erupted into cheers, and even Rafi smiled—a small, shy smile, but a smile nonetheless.

Ms. Lopez approached, clapping her hands. "Well done, everyone!" she said, her voice filled with pride. "You've all worked together beautifully, and I'm so impressed with how you combined your different skills to solve the puzzles and complete the challenges."

As the teams gathered around, celebrating their success, Rafi stayed back a little, still unsure of his place in the group. But Ora wasn't about to let him slip away unnoticed.

She walked over to him, her heart warm with gratitude. "You were amazing, Rafi. This whole scavenger hunt was your idea, and it turned out so great. Everyone loved it."

7 Lessons Learned from Chapter 19:

1. **Inclusion requires patience**: Ora and her friends understood that Rafi needed time to feel comfortable, and they gave him space to participate at his own pace.
2. **Creativity brings people together**: The scavenger hunt, with its mix of puzzles, physical challenges, and creativity, showed

that there are many ways to engage different kinds of kids.

3. **Small steps lead to big breakthroughs**: Rafi's decision to place the final puzzle piece was a small but important step toward him feeling included in the group.

4. **Teamwork shines in diversity**: The scavenger hunt highlighted how different kids' strengths—whether physical, creative, or intellectual—could come together to achieve a common goal.

5. **Acknowledging others builds confidence**: Ora made sure to recognize Rafi's contribution, helping him feel more confident and willing to participate in the future.

6. **Games are about more than winning**: The scavenger hunt wasn't about who finished first, but about how well the teams worked together and supported each other.

7. **Inclusivity is ongoing**: Even after making progress, Ora and her friends knew that there would always be new kids, like Rafi, who needed to feel included, and that their efforts to create a welcoming environment must continue.

Chapter 20: A Playground Celebration

A few days after the scavenger hunt, the playground felt more alive than ever. Kids who had once been reluctant to join the games were now actively participating, and even Rafi had started to engage more with the group. He hadn't yet fully joined in the faster-paced activities, but he contributed to the planning of games and puzzles, and Ora noticed that he was slowly beginning to open up to his classmates.

With everything going so well, Ora and her friends began to think about how they could celebrate the progress they had made. They had worked hard to make the playground more inclusive, creative, and fun, and they wanted to acknowledge how far they had come. One afternoon, as they sat under the big tree during recess, Kiva proposed an idea.

"What if we had a big celebration?" she suggested. "Like a playground party, but with games, activities, and maybe even some special surprises."

Dano nodded enthusiastically. "That sounds awesome! We could bring together all the different kinds of activities we've done—team games, puzzles, creative challenges, and storytelling. And we could invite everyone, not just the regular players."

Remi grinned. "And we could make it a way to thank everyone who's helped us along the way—Ms. Lopez, the teachers, and even the kids who joined in and made the playground what it is now."

Sami, who had been quietly listening, spoke up with a thoughtful expression. "We should call it something special. Like a celebration of everything we've built together—a 'Playground Festival' or something like that."

Ora's eyes lit up at the idea. A Playground Festival! It sounded perfect. They could combine all the different elements that made their playground unique, and it would be a chance for everyone—kids of all abilities, interests, and backgrounds—to come together and celebrate what they had created.

"I love it," Ora said, excitement building in her voice. "A Playground Festival. It'll be a celebration of everything we've accomplished, and it'll show that the playground belongs to all of us."

They began brainstorming ideas for the festival, determined to make it a day to remember. Each of them had different ideas for what should be included:

- **Kiva** wanted to set up a giant obstacle course that would challenge the kids' physical abilities while still allowing everyone to participate, no matter their skill level. She designed it with different paths so that there were easier and more difficult options.
- **Dano** suggested a creative zone where kids could paint, draw, and contribute to the mural wall that had started in the Creative Corner. He wanted to give everyone a chance to express themselves through art and leave their mark on the playground.
- **Remi** proposed a storytelling area, where kids could gather to tell their own stories, perform short skits, or even recite poems they had written. It would be an extension of the Story Circle, but on a bigger scale, with everyone invited to share their creativity.
- **Sami** thought they should have a scavenger hunt similar to the one they had done before, but with even more layers and surprises. It would give the kids who loved puzzles a chance to shine.
- **Ora**, always thinking about how to bring people together, wanted to create a special activity around the Friendship Bench. She suggested that throughout the day, kids could sit

on the bench and talk with someone they hadn't played with before. The goal would be to meet new friends and build even more connections across the playground.

As they discussed their ideas, Ora realized they were missing one key element—Rafi. He had come up with the scavenger hunt idea that had been such a success, and Ora knew he had a lot to offer in planning the festival. She glanced over and saw Rafi sitting nearby, reading a book on the bench.

"Hey, Rafi," Ora called out, walking over to him. "We're planning a Playground Festival, and we'd love to hear your ideas. You came up with such a great scavenger hunt—do you have any thoughts on what we could do for the festival?"

Rafi looked up from his book, clearly surprised to be included in the conversation again. He hesitated for a moment, then closed his book and stood up. "A festival sounds cool," he said quietly. "Maybe you could have a treasure hunt instead of just a scavenger hunt. Something where each team has to find pieces of a map, and when they put it together, it leads to a hidden 'treasure' somewhere on the playground."

Ora smiled. "That's a great idea! A treasure hunt would be so much fun, and it would add a new twist to the scavenger hunt."

Rafi gave a small nod, clearly pleased that his idea had been accepted so readily. "I could help hide the clues if you want," he offered.

"Definitely," Ora said. "We'll need all the help we can get. Thanks, Rafi!"

As the group continued planning, excitement spread across the playground. Word about the festival quickly traveled, and kids began to ask about how they could get involved. Ms. Lopez, always supportive, offered to help the group organize the event and even suggested involving other teachers to spread the word to the whole school.

By the time the day of the Playground Festival arrived, the entire school was buzzing with anticipation. Bright banners hung from the trees, colorful streamers waved in the breeze, and the different zones of the playground had been transformed into activity stations. Kids lined up eagerly for each event, and everywhere Ora looked, there were smiles and laughter.

The **Obstacle Course**, designed by Kiva, was a huge hit. Kids of all ages and abilities tackled the course, with some choosing the more challenging path while others took the easier route. The goal wasn't to race against each other but to finish together, and teams cheered each other on as they made their way through.

In the **Creative Zone**, Dano had set up tables full of paints, markers, and craft supplies. Kids sat together, creating colorful drawings and contributing to the ever-growing mural wall. Some painted animals, others created abstract designs, and a few kids even added messages of kindness and friendship to the mural.

The **Storytelling Area** was full of kids listening intently as their classmates shared stories, poems, and short performances. Althea, always eager to tell a good tale, stood proudly in front of the group, weaving an exciting adventure story that had everyone on the edge of their seats.

The **Treasure Hunt**, designed with Rafi's help, was a thrilling adventure. Teams searched all over the playground for pieces of the treasure map, working together to solve the clues and uncover the hidden treasure—a box filled with fun toys and snacks for everyone to share. Rafi had hidden the clues so well that even the older kids found themselves stumped at times, but eventually, the teams worked together to put the pieces of the map together.

Perhaps the most meaningful part of the day was at the **Friendship Bench**, where Ora's idea of encouraging kids to meet new friends took off in unexpected ways. Kids who hadn't played together before sat down on the bench and struck up conversations, discovering common interests and new friendships. Some of the older kids who had once resisted the changes were now sitting beside younger students, sharing stories and laughs.

7 Lessons Learned from Chapter 20:

1. **Celebrating progress brings people together**: The Playground Festival was a way to celebrate all the hard work that went into making the playground more inclusive, giving kids a sense of pride and accomplishment.
2. **Inclusivity takes many forms**: The festival featured a variety of activities—physical, creative, and social—showing that inclusion means offering something for everyone, no matter their interests or abilities.
3. **New friendships can grow from shared experiences**: The Friendship Bench activity allowed kids who hadn't interacted before to make new friends, fostering deeper connections.
4. **Small contributions make a big impact**: Rafi's idea for the treasure hunt added excitement to the festival, showing that every kid's input is valuable in building a fun, inclusive environment.
5. **Leadership can come from unexpected places**: Throughout the festival, different kids took on leadership roles, demonstrating that everyone has the potential to lead in their own way.
6. **Community is built through shared effort**: The festival was a team effort, and the kids learned that working together to create something special brings the entire community closer.
7. **Inclusivity is worth celebrating**: The Playground Festival was more than just a party—it was a recognition of the importance of inclusivity and the joy that comes from creating a space where everyone feels welcome.

Chapter 21: The New Playground Equipment

The day after the Playground Festival, the kids of Sunnyhill Elementary were still buzzing with excitement. The event had been a huge success, and the entire school was talking about it. However, the excitement wasn't just about the festival. Something even bigger was on the horizon: the arrival of new playground equipment.

For weeks, Ora and her friends had heard whispers that the school was getting new equipment—things like accessible swings, ramps, and sensory play areas designed for kids of all abilities. Ms. Lopez had mentioned that the school had approved the changes based on the feedback from the students, and the new equipment was set to arrive soon. The idea that their efforts had sparked such a big change was almost too good to be true.

As the days passed, anticipation built. The teachers didn't say exactly when the new equipment would arrive, but every morning, the kids ran to the playground, hoping to see the start of construction. And then, one bright Monday morning, it happened.

Ora arrived at school to see trucks parked near the playground, and construction workers were busy unloading pieces of brightly colored equipment. Some kids gathered near the fence, trying to get a glimpse of what was coming, and Ora felt a wave of excitement as she spotted a new swing set, but this one was different—it had wide, supportive seats that were perfect for kids who needed extra stability. There were also ramps being built, allowing kids with wheelchairs, like Althea, to easily access more parts of the playground. A new sensory play area was being installed as well, with textured surfaces, musical instruments, and colorful panels that were designed to engage kids in different ways.

Ora ran over to find her friends already watching in awe. Kiva, Sami, Dano, Remi, and Althea were all gathered near the edge of the playground, grinning from ear to ear.

"Look at all this!" Kiva said, pointing at the new equipment. "It's even better than we imagined!"

Sami nodded. "I can't wait to try out the new sensory area. It looks like it'll be really fun for everyone."

Althea, who had been smiling quietly as she watched the workers build the ramps, turned to Ora. "I never thought I'd see the day when I could actually use all the parts of the playground," she said, her voice full of gratitude. "It's amazing."

"It's incredible," Ora agreed, her heart swelling with pride. "I can't believe how far we've come. Remember when we first started, just trying to make sure everyone could play together? Now look at this—it's a playground for everyone."

Ms. Lopez approached the group with a big smile. "Good morning, everyone! I see you're just as excited as I am. The school board was so impressed with everything you've done to create a more inclusive playground, they decided to invest in these changes. And it's all thanks to your hard work and dedication."

Ora felt a warm glow of pride at Ms. Lopez's words. They had started with small changes—games and activities to include everyone—but now the playground itself was changing to reflect their vision. It was becoming a place where every child, regardless of ability, could feel welcome and fully participate.

The construction took a few days, and during that time, the kids watched eagerly as the new equipment took shape. Every day, something new appeared—another piece of the puzzle that would make their playground more inclusive. The sensory play area was especially exciting. It included musical instruments like chimes and drums, which allowed kids to create sounds and rhythms as they played. There were textured walls and paths that kids could touch and explore, offering a completely different kind of play experience for those who preferred sensory activities over physical challenges.

Finally, the day arrived when the new equipment was ready to be used. The playground had been transformed, and Ora could hardly believe her eyes as she and her friends gathered for the official ribbon-cutting ceremony. The principal, Mr. Wilkins, stood at the front of the group, holding a pair of oversized scissors, while the kids gathered around, buzzing with excitement.

"Today is a very special day," Mr. Wilkins said, his voice booming across the playground. "Thanks to the ideas and leadership of our students, particularly Ora and her friends, we've made our playground a place where everyone can play, learn, and have fun—together. These changes wouldn't have happened without their commitment to inclusivity, and we're so proud of what they've accomplished."

He gestured toward the new equipment, and the kids cheered. Mr. Wilkins handed the scissors to Ora, giving her the honor of cutting the ribbon. Ora felt her heart racing with excitement as she stepped forward, her friends cheering her on. With one swift snip, the ribbon fell, and the playground was officially open.

The kids raced to try out the new equipment, and the energy was infectious. Althea, grinning from ear to ear, wheeled herself up the new ramp and finally reached the top of the jungle gym, where she could now interact with the other kids playing there. Finn and Vex were already testing out the new obstacle course, which had been designed with multiple difficulty levels, ensuring that kids of all abilities could participate. Sami, always curious about new things, headed straight for the sensory area, where he began experimenting with the musical instruments and textured panels.

Ora and her friends stood back for a moment, watching the joyful chaos unfold. It was everything they had dreamed of and more. Kids of all abilities were laughing, playing, and exploring the new playground together, and no one was left out.

"This is amazing," Remi said, her voice full of wonder. "It's like everything we worked for has finally come together."

"I know," Ora said, smiling as she watched Althea at the top of the jungle gym, waving down at them. "It's everything we wanted—a place where every kid feels like they belong."

As the day went on, Ora and her friends explored the new playground, trying out all the new equipment and games. The sensory area was a big hit, especially with some of the younger kids who loved the bright colors and the interactive elements. The accessible swings were constantly in use, with kids of all abilities taking turns, and the ramps allowed everyone to navigate the playground with ease.

Later that afternoon, as the sun began to set and the kids started heading home, Ora sat on the Friendship Bench, feeling a deep sense of fulfillment. She thought back to the first time they had talked about making changes to the playground. Back then, it had seemed like such a big task—how could a few kids really make a difference? But now, looking at the transformed playground, Ora realized that they had done more than just make a difference. They had changed the entire culture of their school.

As she sat there, Rafi approached and sat down next to her. He had been participating more lately, and Ora was glad to see how much he had come out of his shell. The treasure hunt at the festival had been a huge success, and Rafi had started offering more ideas for games and activities.

"It's pretty cool, isn't it?" Rafi said, looking out at the playground.

7 Lessons Learned from Chapter 21:

1. **Change is possible when people work together**: The new playground equipment was a direct result of the kids' efforts to create an inclusive environment, showing that even small actions can lead to big changes.

2. **Inclusivity benefits everyone**: The new equipment made the

playground more accessible, allowing all kids—regardless of their abilities—to participate and have fun.

3. **Celebrating success is important**: The ribbon-cutting ceremony was a way to acknowledge the hard work that went into transforming the playground and to celebrate the progress they had made.

4. **Every kid has a role to play**: Whether it was Rafi's treasure hunt idea or Althea's determination to reach the top of the jungle gym, every kid contributed to making the playground better for everyone.

5. **Leadership can come from anywhere**: Ora and her friends led the charge to create an inclusive playground, but along the way, other kids, like Rafi, stepped up and made their own contributions.

6. **New challenges bring new opportunities**: The new playground equipment opened up new ways to play, creating opportunities for all kids to explore their abilities and interests.

7. **Inclusivity is ongoing**: While the new equipment was a big step forward, Ora and her friends knew that their efforts to create an inclusive community would continue, welcoming new kids and new ideas along the way.

Chapter 22: Facing New Challenges

With the new playground equipment in place and the success of the Playground Festival fresh in everyone's mind, Sunnyhill Elementary felt more unified than ever. The playground had become a symbol of inclusivity, creativity, and friendship—a place where every kid could find something they loved. But as the weeks went on, Ora and her friends realized that maintaining an inclusive environment wasn't always easy. There were still challenges, some more subtle than before, that they hadn't anticipated.

It started one afternoon when Sami came over to Ora during recess, looking upset. He had just finished playing in the sensory area with some of the younger kids, and Ora could tell something was bothering him.

"Hey, Sami. What's wrong?" Ora asked, concerned.

Sami sighed and sat down beside Ora on the edge of the jungle gym. "I don't know. It's just...some of the older kids don't want to play in the sensory area. They're making fun of it, saying it's 'baby stuff.' I heard a couple of them telling the younger kids that it's not for them."

Ora frowned. She hadn't expected this. The sensory area had been such a hit when it was first installed, with kids of all ages exploring the musical instruments, textures, and interactive elements. But now, it seemed like some of the older kids were trying to separate themselves from the others, labeling the sensory area as something only the younger kids could use.

"That's not right," Ora said, feeling frustration build. "The whole point of the new equipment was that it's for *everyone*. It's not just for certain ages. We've worked so hard to make sure everyone feels included."

Sami nodded. "I know. But it feels like some kids still don't get it. They're acting like the playground is only for certain types of play. I

even heard one of the kids say the sensory area was boring compared to
the obstacle course."

Ora's mind raced as she tried to think of a solution. This was a
new kind of problem—one they hadn't faced before. It wasn't about
excluding kids from games anymore; it was about kids making
assumptions about what kinds of activities were "cool" or "uncool." If
they didn't address it, the playground could once again become a place
where some kids felt left out.

Later that day, Ora gathered her friends under the big tree to
discuss what Sami had told her. They all sat in a circle, the sun filtering
through the leaves above them.

"We need to talk about something," Ora began, glancing at Sami
for support. "Sami told me that some of the older kids are making fun
of the sensory area, saying it's just for younger kids. It's causing some
of the younger ones to feel like they don't belong there anymore. And
it's not just the sensory area—there's this attitude going around that
certain parts of the playground are 'cooler' than others."

Remi sighed. "Ugh, I hate that. It's like we're going backward,
separating parts of the playground by age or what's 'fun' and what's
not."

Dano, always thoughtful, nodded. "Yeah, and it's not just about
age, either. Some kids who are quieter or don't like the more physical
activities are being pushed out of the games, even if they want to join."

Kiva crossed her arms, frowning. "We can't let that happen. We've
worked too hard to let the playground go back to being divided like it
was before."

"We need to find a way to show everyone that every part of the
playground is for *everyone*," Ora said firmly. "No one should feel like
they don't belong in certain spaces just because of their age or what they
like to do."

The group brainstormed ideas for how to tackle the problem. They
didn't want to come across as bossy or force anyone to do something

they didn't enjoy, but they needed to send a clear message that the playground was for all kids, and that every activity was valuable in its own way.

After some discussion, Sami came up with a brilliant idea.

"What if we had a day where everyone tries something new?" he suggested. "Like, we could call it 'Mix-it-Up Day.' We'd encourage kids to play in parts of the playground they don't usually go to. The older kids could spend time in the sensory area, and the younger ones could try out the obstacle course or the jungle gym. We could make it fun by turning it into a challenge—kind of like a scavenger hunt, but with different activities."

Ora's eyes lit up. "That's a great idea, Sami! It would give everyone a chance to experience different parts of the playground and realize that all the areas are fun in their own way."

Kiva grinned. "And we could have different teams, mixing up older and younger kids, so they have to work together. It'll show that no part of the playground is 'just for certain kids.' It's for all of us."

With the plan set, the group spent the next few days preparing for **Mix-it-Up Day.** They made colorful posters to hang around the school, explaining the idea: a day where everyone would explore different parts of the playground and try new activities, all while working together in mixed-age teams. The goal was to encourage kids to see the value in every part of the playground, from the sensory area to the obstacle course, and to break down the invisible walls that were starting to form.

When the day finally arrived, Ora and her friends were nervous but hopeful. They had spent a lot of time planning, and they knew that if this worked, it could help bring the playground community even closer.

The first challenge of the day involved the sensory area. Ora's team, which included a mix of older and younger kids, gathered around the colorful instruments and textured surfaces. At first, some of the older kids looked hesitant, but Ora encouraged them to give it a try.

"Remember, this is all about trying something new," she said with a smile. "You might be surprised by how much fun it is!"

Finn, who was usually more interested in physical challenges, picked up a set of chimes and tapped them experimentally. To his surprise, the soft, melodic sounds that followed caught his attention. He tapped the chimes again, this time with more rhythm, and soon the younger kids joined in, creating a spontaneous musical performance.

"This is actually kind of cool," Finn admitted, smiling as the younger kids clapped along to the beat.

Across the playground, in the obstacle course, Althea's team was working on a physical challenge that involved navigating through the course in creative ways. Some of the younger kids were nervous about trying it out, but Althea, who was known for her encouragement, led the way, showing them that the course was about more than just strength—it was about strategy and teamwork.

"Let's take it slow and steady," Althea called out as her team moved through the course. "It's not about who's the fastest; it's about how we can work together to get everyone through."

7 Lessons Learned from Chapter 22:

1. **Inclusivity requires constant effort**: Even when progress is made, it's important to stay vigilant and address new challenges that arise, like kids feeling excluded from certain parts of the playground.

2. **Breaking down stereotypes is important**: Some kids viewed the sensory area as "just for younger kids," but Mix-it-Up Day showed that all parts of the playground can be enjoyed by everyone.

3. **Trying new things can lead to unexpected fun**: Finn discovered that playing in the sensory area was more fun than he expected, reminding everyone that stepping out of your comfort zone can be rewarding.

4. **Age doesn't define play**: The playground is for all ages, and mixing older and younger kids together helps break down barriers and fosters teamwork and understanding.

5. **Leaders come in all forms**: Althea showed that leadership isn't just about being the fastest or strongest—it's about encouraging others and helping everyone succeed.

6. **Community is built through shared experiences**: Mix-it-Up Day brought the kids together by having them try new activities, reminding them that they're all part of the same community, no matter what they like to do.

7. **Inclusivity is an ongoing journey**: Ora and her friends learned that creating a welcoming environment takes ongoing effort, and they were prepared to keep working to make the playground better for everyone.

Chapter 23: New Faces, New Challenges

The success of Mix-it-Up Day had reaffirmed what Ora and her friends already knew: the playground was evolving into something truly special. However, with the arrival of the new playground equipment and the growing reputation of Sunnyhill Elementary as a place where every kid was welcome, the school began to attract new students. And while this was exciting, it also brought with it new challenges.

One morning, about a month after Mix-it-Up Day, Ora noticed a group of unfamiliar faces during recess. She recognized some of them as new kids who had recently transferred to Sunnyhill. There were a few younger kids who immediately gravitated toward the playground's sensory area, a few older ones who looked curious but kept to themselves, and one boy who stood apart from everyone else, not engaging at all. He seemed frustrated, his arms crossed as he watched the other kids play. Ora's natural instinct to include everyone kicked in, and she knew she had to reach out.

The boy's name was Malik, and Ora had seen him sitting alone a few times during lunch, always looking unhappy. Today was no different. He stood near the swings, watching, but making no move to join. Ora made a mental note to approach him after checking in with some of the other new students.

After helping a few younger kids get acquainted with the new obstacle course and introducing them to her friends, Ora finally made her way over to Malik. She could feel the tension radiating off him before she even reached him. He wasn't just shy like Rafi had been when he first arrived—he seemed upset, maybe even angry.

"Hey, Malik," Ora said gently, stopping a few feet away so she didn't crowd him. "I noticed you've been hanging out by yourself. Do you want to join us? We're about to start a new game, and I think you'd be really good at it."

Malik looked at her, his dark eyes narrowing slightly. "I'm fine here," he muttered, kicking at the dirt.

Ora frowned, sensing that something deeper was going on. "Are you sure? We're playing a game that's really fun. And if games aren't your thing, we have a bunch of other activities too. There's the sensory area, the creative corner—you could help us design something new if you want."

Malik's expression darkened. "I don't want to play any of your games," he said, his voice sharp. "This playground is dumb. I liked my old school better."

Ora felt a pang of sympathy. Malik had only recently moved to Sunnyhill, and it was clear he was having a hard time adjusting. But his outright rejection of the playground stung. After all the hard work she and her friends had done to make the playground welcoming, it hurt to hear someone dismiss it like that.

"I get that moving to a new school is hard," Ora said carefully. "It takes time to get used to things, but we've worked really hard to make this playground a place where everyone can find something they like. Maybe we just haven't found the right thing for you yet."

Malik shrugged, clearly uninterested in engaging further. "Like I said, I'm fine here."

Ora wanted to push more, to convince him to at least give the playground a chance, but she knew that wouldn't help. She had learned from Rafi that sometimes people needed time and space to open up. She decided not to push any further for now.

"Well, if you change your mind, we're always here," Ora said, keeping her tone light. "You're welcome to join anytime."

With that, Ora walked away, feeling a little discouraged. Malik wasn't like the other kids who had eventually come around. He didn't seem interested in anything they were doing, and worse, he was dismissing everything they had worked so hard to create. It wasn't just that he didn't want to play—he seemed to actively dislike the playground itself.

Ora shared her worries with her friends later that day, as they sat under the big tree during lunch. They all listened intently, nodding in understanding.

"It sounds like he's going through a tough time," Kiva said thoughtfully. "Maybe it's not really about the playground. He might just be frustrated about being in a new place."

Sami, who had experienced a similar adjustment when he first moved to Sunnyhill, chimed in. "Yeah, it can be really hard moving to a new school, especially if you liked your old one. I felt the same way when I first came here. I didn't like anything at first because I missed my old friends and my old school."

Remi agreed. "He probably just needs time. But it's hard because he's not just ignoring the playground—he's rejecting it. It's like he's angry that we're all having fun, and he's not part of it."

Ora sighed. "I don't want to give up on him. But I don't know how to help him without making him feel like we're forcing him to join in."

Dano, who had been quiet, spoke up. "Maybe we don't start by getting him to join a game. What if we just try talking to him more? Like, really listen to what's bothering him. If we can understand why he's upset, maybe we can help him feel more comfortable."

Ora thought about Dano's suggestion and realized he was right. They had been so focused on including Malik in the games that they hadn't stopped to really listen to what was bothering him. If they wanted to make progress, they needed to understand his perspective.

The next day, Ora decided to approach Malik again, but this time with a different plan. She didn't mention the playground or the games. Instead, she simply walked over and sat down next to him on the bench near the swings.

"Hey," Ora said, her voice soft. "I won't ask you to play again. But I was wondering—what was your old school like? What did you like about it?"

Malik glanced at her, his expression suspicious, but after a moment, he shrugged. "It was different. The playground wasn't like this. We didn't have all these fancy games and stuff."

Ora nodded, encouraging him to continue. "What did you do there?"

Malik hesitated, then sighed. "We played a lot of sports. Soccer, mostly. And there wasn't all this 'everyone has to play together' stuff. You could just do your own thing. It was more...normal."

Ora listened carefully, realizing that Malik's frustration came from missing the freedom and competitiveness of his old school's playground. He wasn't used to the collaborative, inclusive games that Ora and her friends had created. He missed the simplicity of just kicking a ball around, where things weren't so focused on making sure everyone was involved.

"I get that," Ora said after a moment. "It sounds like you really loved the way things worked at your old school. It's tough when you come somewhere new and everything's different. It can feel like you don't fit in."

Malik looked down at his hands, his tough exterior starting to soften just a little. "Yeah," he muttered. "It's just...I don't want to do all these weird games. I just want to play soccer."

Ora smiled gently. "That's fair. And you know what? We can play soccer too. The point of this playground isn't just to make everyone play one way. It's about making sure everyone has a chance to do what they like. If soccer is what you want to play, we can totally do that."

Malik's eyes flicked up, surprised. "Really?"

"Of course," Ora said. "We want everyone to have fun. If soccer is your thing, then let's set up a game. You don't have to join the other stuff if you don't want to."

For the first time since she had met him, Malik's expression softened into something like relief. "Okay," he said, his voice tentative. "Maybe we can try it."

7 Lessons Learned from Chapter 23:

1. **Listening is the first step to understanding**: Ora learned that truly listening to Malik's concerns helped her understand his frustration, which allowed her to address the problem in a way that worked for him.

2. **Inclusion doesn't mean forcing everyone to do the same thing**: Ora realized that including Malik meant allowing him to do what he loved—playing soccer—rather than pushing him to join the games he didn't enjoy.

3. **Different preferences are okay**: Not every kid enjoys the same activities, and that's okay. The key is to make space for everyone to enjoy what they love.

4. **Adapting to change can be hard**: Malik's difficulty adjusting to the new school and playground showed that change can be tough, and it's important to be patient with those who are struggling.

5. **Inclusivity means flexibility**: By being flexible and willing to try something different, Ora and her friends were able to make Malik feel more comfortable and included.

6. **New friendships take time**: Malik didn't open up right away, but with patience and understanding, he began to feel like part of the group.

7. **Respecting others' interests builds trust**: Ora's willingness to play soccer with Malik showed him that his interests were respected, which helped build trust and opened the door to further inclusion.

Chapter 24: Growing Pains

Malik's gradual integration into the playground community was a victory for Ora and her friends. They had learned to meet him where he was, allowing him to play soccer and easing him into the group on his own terms. But as much as Malik was starting to fit in, Ora began to notice new challenges bubbling beneath the surface of their growing playground community.

The increase in new students meant more diverse interests and personalities to accommodate, and while that diversity had once felt like a blessing, it was beginning to cause friction. Some kids were still drawn to the structured games like *Skill Quest* and *Treasure Island,* while others, like Malik, preferred the freedom of simpler games like soccer. And then there were those who loved the sensory area, the storytelling circle, or the Creative Corner, where they could draw, paint, and tell stories. With so many different activities happening at once, the playground started to feel a bit...disconnected.

It wasn't just the variety of activities that was creating tension. Ora had overheard a few conversations during recess that made her uneasy.

"I don't want to play with the younger kids anymore," Finn had said to Vex one afternoon. "They slow us down in the obstacle course."

Vex had nodded in agreement. "Yeah, it's not fun when we can't really compete because we have to wait for them."

Ora had also heard one of the newer kids, a girl named Leila, talking to her friends by the Friendship Bench.

"Why do we always have to play these weird games?" Leila had said, sounding frustrated. "I just want to do my own thing without having to be part of a team all the time."

That afternoon, Ora sat under the big tree, feeling the weight of these growing frustrations. She knew that things weren't as harmonious as they had once been, and it worried her. The playground was supposed to be a place where everyone could feel included, but now it felt like kids were starting to drift into separate groups again, preferring to stick with activities they were most comfortable with rather than trying new things or playing with different kids.

Kiva, Sami, Dano, and Remi joined her after recess, each of them noticing the same things Ora had.

"It feels like the playground's getting too big for us to handle," Kiva said, leaning back against the tree. "There are so many kids now, and they all want to do different things. It's hard to keep everyone together."

Sami nodded. "Yeah, I've heard some of the older kids complaining about the younger ones, and even some of the newer kids are starting to avoid the games we set up. I don't know how to keep everyone happy."

Dano, always thoughtful, added, "It's like we're trying to be everything to everyone, and it's making it harder to keep the playground united. I don't think it's about the games anymore—it's about the groups forming around them."

Ora sighed. "I know what you mean. It feels like the playground is dividing again, but not in the same way as before. Now it's not about who gets to play, but about what people want to play. I don't want anyone to feel left out, but I also don't want kids to feel like they have to do things they don't enjoy."

Remi spoke up, her voice calm but serious. "Maybe the problem is that we're trying to organize everything too much. We set up these big group games because we wanted everyone to play together, but maybe that's not what everyone wants anymore. Some kids might just need space to do their own thing."

Ora considered this, feeling conflicted. Remi had a point—maybe they had been too focused on making sure everyone played together. But the idea of letting the playground return to being divided by cliques didn't sit right with her either.

"I get what you're saying," Ora said slowly. "But I don't want to go back to the days when only certain kids felt like they could play in certain areas. We worked so hard to make the playground a place where everyone could feel welcome, and I don't want to lose that."

Dano scratched his head thoughtfully. "Maybe there's a way to do both. Like, we could create spaces for different kinds of play, but still encourage kids to move between them. That way, if someone wants to play soccer, they can, but they should also feel welcome to join a group game or try out the sensory area if they want."

Kiva nodded in agreement. "Yeah, it doesn't have to be all or nothing. We could let the playground be more flexible—give kids the freedom to choose what they want to do, but make sure they know they're welcome in all the spaces."

Ora felt a small flicker of hope. Maybe this was the solution—creating a more flexible, open-ended playground that allowed kids to choose their activities without feeling pressured to stick with one group or another. It wouldn't be easy, but it might be the only way to keep the playground inclusive without forcing everyone into the same mold.

That afternoon, Ora and her friends began sketching out a new plan for the playground. They decided to create a **Playground Passport**—a simple, fun way to encourage kids to try different activities across the playground while still allowing them the freedom to play what they loved. The passport would have different zones listed—*Physical Play* (like soccer or the obstacle course), *Creative Play* (like the Creative Corner and Storytelling), and *Team Games* (like *Skill Quest* and *Treasure Island*). Each kid could earn stamps or stickers for participating in activities in each zone, and once they filled their passport with enough stamps, they'd earn a small prize, like a special sticker or a badge of recognition from Ms. Lopez.

"We won't force anyone to play a game they don't like," Sami explained as they worked on the idea, "but the passport will give kids a reason to explore other parts of the playground and try new things. And the prizes will be small, but enough to encourage participation."

Ora liked the idea. It was gentle, non-intrusive, and still aligned with their goal of inclusivity. The passport wouldn't force kids to play together, but it would nudge them in that direction.

The next day, they presented the idea to Ms. Lopez, who was enthusiastic about the plan.

"This is a wonderful idea," Ms. Lopez said, smiling as she looked at the colorful mock-ups of the Playground Passports the group had designed. "I think this could be a great way to keep the spirit of inclusivity alive while allowing for more individual choice. Let's try it out!"

Ms. Lopez helped Ora and her friends organize the distribution of the passports during recess that day. They gathered the kids by the big tree and explained how the passports worked. The response was overwhelmingly positive—most of the kids were excited to earn stamps and try different activities, while others, like Malik, were relieved that they could still do what they loved without feeling pressured to join in everything.

"Okay, everyone!" Ora called out to the group. "The Playground Passport is a fun way to explore different parts of the playground, but remember, it's all about having fun. You don't have to rush to fill it up—just enjoy trying new things!"

As the kids dispersed, passports in hand, Ora watched them with a mixture of hope and anticipation. This was a new chapter for the playground—one that would allow for more flexibility while still fostering a sense of community. She wasn't sure if it would solve all the problems, but it felt like a step in the right direction.

7 Lessons Learned from Chapter 24:

1. **Inclusivity doesn't mean everyone has to do the same thing**: The Playground Passport encouraged kids to explore different activities without forcing them to participate in games they didn't enjoy.

2. **Flexibility is key to keeping a community together**: Allowing kids to choose their own activities while still encouraging them to try new things helped maintain a sense of unity on the playground.

3. **Fostering curiosity leads to growth**: The Playground Passport system sparked curiosity in the kids, encouraging them to step outside their comfort zones and try new activities.

4. **Inclusivity requires ongoing adaptation**: As the playground community grew, Ora and her friends had to adapt their approach to keep everyone included and engaged.

5. **Small rewards can motivate big changes**: The simple reward system of earning stamps and prizes motivated kids to explore parts of the playground they hadn't tried before.

6. **Leadership comes in different forms**: Finn's growth as a leader, helping younger kids through the obstacle course, showed that leadership isn't just about competition—it's about supporting others.

7. **Patience and understanding go a long way**: Ora and her friends learned that being patient with kids like Malik, who were reluctant to join, paid off in the long run as he slowly became more involved.

Chapter 25: A Playground for the Future

As the school year began to wind down and the weather grew warmer, the playground at Sunnyhill Elementary became the center of activity. Every day after lunch, kids rushed outside to fill their **Playground Passports**, explore new activities, and enjoy the inclusive environment that Ora and her friends had worked so hard to create. The Passport system had proven to be a great success, encouraging kids to try out different zones while still allowing them the freedom to play their favorite games.

But despite all the progress they had made, Ora knew there was still work to do. The playground was constantly evolving, and with each new challenge, Ora learned that inclusivity wasn't something you achieved once—it was something you had to keep working on. As more new students arrived and the playground continued to grow, the importance of staying flexible and open to change became even clearer.

One afternoon, as Ora sat under the big tree with her friends, watching the kids play, Ms. Lopez approached the group with a thoughtful expression. She had been their biggest supporter throughout the playground's transformation, always encouraging their ideas and helping them implement changes. But today, Ora could tell that Ms. Lopez had something important on her mind.

"Hey, Ms. Lopez," Ora said, smiling up at her teacher. "What's up?"

Ms. Lopez sat down on the grass beside them, glancing around at the bustling playground. "I've been thinking about everything you've accomplished this year," she said. "The Playground Passport, the new equipment, the way you've made sure every kid feels included. It's been truly inspiring to watch."

Ora and her friends exchanged proud smiles. They were proud of what they had built, but they also knew Ms. Lopez wouldn't bring this up just to give them compliments.

"But," Ms. Lopez continued, her tone gentle, "I also think there's an opportunity here to make an even bigger impact."

Kiva tilted her head, curious. "What do you mean?"

"Well," Ms. Lopez said, "you've created something wonderful here at Sunnyhill, but I know that other schools in our district—and beyond—could benefit from what you've learned. What if you shared your story, your ideas, and the systems you've created with other schools? You could inspire kids in other places to make their playgrounds more inclusive, just like you did here."

The idea hit Ora like a bolt of lightning. It hadn't occurred to her that what they had built at Sunnyhill could spread beyond their own school. She had always thought of their work as something local—just for their playground. But what if they could help other schools, other kids, create the same kind of inclusive environments?

"That's...that's an amazing idea," Ora said, excitement rising in her chest. "But how would we do that? How would we share what we've done?"

Ms. Lopez smiled warmly. "I'm glad you're excited about it! I've spoken with the school district, and they're interested in hearing from you all. They'd like you to put together a presentation about the work you've done, including the Playground Passport and the new equipment. You'd be speaking to principals and teachers from other schools, and maybe even some student leaders. If they like your ideas, they could adopt them at their own schools."

Remi's eyes widened. "We'd be speaking to principals? That sounds huge!"

"It is," Ms. Lopez agreed. "But I believe in you. You've done something special here, and I think it's time to share it with the world."

Ora felt a rush of excitement but also a hint of nervousness. The idea of sharing their story with other schools was thrilling, but it also felt like a big responsibility. She glanced at her friends, who looked equally excited and a little overwhelmed.

"We could do this," Dano said, his voice steady. "We already know what works and what doesn't. We just have to tell our story—how we started, what changes we made, and how it helped bring the playground together."

Sami nodded. "Yeah, and we can explain the Passport system. It's a simple idea, but it's made a big difference. If other schools used it, they could make their playgrounds more inclusive too."

Kiva grinned, her usual enthusiasm bubbling to the surface. "And we could talk about the new equipment! The sensory area, the accessible swings, the ramps. All of that stuff has made a huge impact here. Imagine if other schools had that too."

Ora took a deep breath, feeling her nervousness fade as her friends spoke. They could do this. They had already accomplished so much at Sunnyhill, and now it was time to take what they had learned and share it with the world.

"Okay," Ora said, her voice confident. "Let's do it. Let's put together a presentation and show other schools how they can make their playgrounds a place for everyone."

Over the next few weeks, Ora and her friends worked closely with Ms. Lopez to create their presentation. They started by mapping out the story of how it all began—how they had noticed that not everyone felt welcome on the playground, and how that had sparked the idea for inclusive games like *Skill Quest* and *Treasure Island*. They explained how the games had brought kids together but also highlighted the need for new equipment, like the accessible swings and ramps. Then they shared the success of Mix-it-Up Day and the Playground Passport, showing how these initiatives had encouraged kids to explore different activities and break down barriers.

To make the presentation more engaging, they included photos and videos from the playground, showing the kids playing together in different zones. There were clips of Finn helping the younger kids through the obstacle course, Althea leading her team through a puzzle challenge, and even Rafi, once reluctant to join in, now participating in a soccer game with a smile on his face.

As the day of the presentation approached, Ora felt a mixture of excitement and nerves. This was bigger than anything they had done before, but she knew they were ready. They had created something special at Sunnyhill, and now it was time to share it with the world.

The presentation took place at the district office, with principals, teachers, and even a few student leaders from other schools in attendance. Ms. Lopez stood proudly by their side as Ora and her friends took turns speaking, sharing their story with the room.

Kiva kicked things off with her usual energy, explaining how the playground had been divided at first, and how they had worked to bring everyone together. Dano talked about the importance of flexibility and allowing kids to explore different kinds of play. Sami shared how the Playground Passport had motivated kids to try new activities, and Remi emphasized how inclusivity had become a core value on the playground. Ora wrapped things up by talking about the impact of the new equipment and the way it had opened up the playground to kids of all abilities.

When they finished, the room erupted in applause. Ora could hardly believe it—they had done it. They had shared their story, and it had resonated with the audience.

After the presentation, several principals and teachers approached them with questions, eager to learn more about how they could implement similar ideas at their own schools. One principal from a nearby school said she was already making plans to create a sensory area, and another teacher mentioned that her school would be adopting the Playground Passport system.

As they left the district office that afternoon, Ora and her friends were buzzing with excitement.

"I can't believe it," Remi said, grinning. "Other schools are actually going to use our ideas!"

"I know," Sami added, shaking his head in disbelief. "It feels unreal."

Ora smiled, feeling a deep sense of accomplishment. "We did it. We really made a difference."

Ms. Lopez beamed at them. "You should all be so proud of yourselves. You've not only changed your own school—you're helping kids across the district. And who knows? Maybe this will spread even further."

As they walked back to school together, Ora thought about how far they had come. What had started as a simple idea to make the playground more inclusive had grown into something much bigger. They had faced challenges, setbacks, and moments of doubt, but they had never given up. And now, their vision was spreading beyond Sunnyhill, helping other schools create playgrounds where every kid felt welcome.

7 Lessons Learned from Chapter 25:

1. **Small ideas can lead to big changes**: What started as a simple desire to make the playground more inclusive grew into a movement that spread beyond Sunnyhill Elementary.

2. **Inclusivity is an ongoing process**: Ora and her friends learned that creating an inclusive environment requires constant effort, adaptation, and a willingness to listen to others.

3. **Sharing success can inspire others**: By sharing their story with other schools, Ora and her friends were able to spread their ideas and help other kids experience the same sense of belonging.

4. **Collaboration leads to stronger communities**: Working together as a team allowed Ora and her friends to achieve more than they could have on their own.

5. **Leadership is about lifting others up**: Ora and her friends didn't just lead by example—they created opportunities for

every kid to feel included and valued.

6. **Inclusivity benefits everyone**: The changes on the playground didn't just help a few kids—they brought the entire community closer together.

7. **A sense of belonging is priceless**: Ultimately, the playground became a place where every kid could find their place, making it more than just a place to play—it became a community.

Don't miss out!

Visit the website below and you can sign up to receive emails whenever Willow Stone publishes a new book. There's no charge and no obligation.

https://books2read.com/r/B-A-LTOLC-OYRBF

BOOKS 2 READ

Connecting independent readers to independent writers.

Did you love *The Day the Playground Became Everyone's Place*? Then you should read *Learning to Forgive and Grow Stronger Together*[1] by Hazel Brook!

In Learning to Forgive and Grow Stronger Together, a group of friends—Aeliana, Zephyr, Fern, Wren, and Thallo—embark on a journey of friendship, self-discovery, and courage. Through the challenges they face, from confronting personal fears to navigating school projects, each friend learns valuable lessons about forgiveness, trust, and finding strength in themselves and each other. With heartwarming stories and relatable characters, this book shows children the importance of empathy, resilience, and teamwork. Perfect for readers ages 5-10, it's a celebration of the power of friendship and the beauty of growing together.

---

1. https://books2read.com/u/mq57Le

2. https://books2read.com/u/mq57Le

Also by Willow Stone

About the Author

Willow Stone writes bedtime stories that captivate children with a unique blend of mystery and calm. Her tales are like soft, whispered secrets of the night, leading little ones into dreamlike realms where the line between waking and sleeping blurs. With a talent for evoking wonder through gentle, imaginative narratives, Willow creates an atmosphere of quiet magic that soothes restless minds and turns bedtime into an enchanting ritual filled with comfort and discovery.

The Good Child

Inspiring values and fellowship

About the Publisher

The Good Child Academy is a premier publisher dedicated to creating enchanting and educational children's books that inspire imagination and creativity. With a focus on delivering high-quality stories, the academy collaborates with talented authors and illustrators to produce books that captivate young minds. Specializing in themes like adventure, learning, and seasonal celebrations such as Halloween, Good Child Academy ensures that each book fosters curiosity, empathy, and a love for reading. Their mission is to nurture the next generation of lifelong readers.

Read more at https://www.patreon.com/thegoodchild/shop.